A BOOK OF TALL STORIES

for Laura with my best wishes

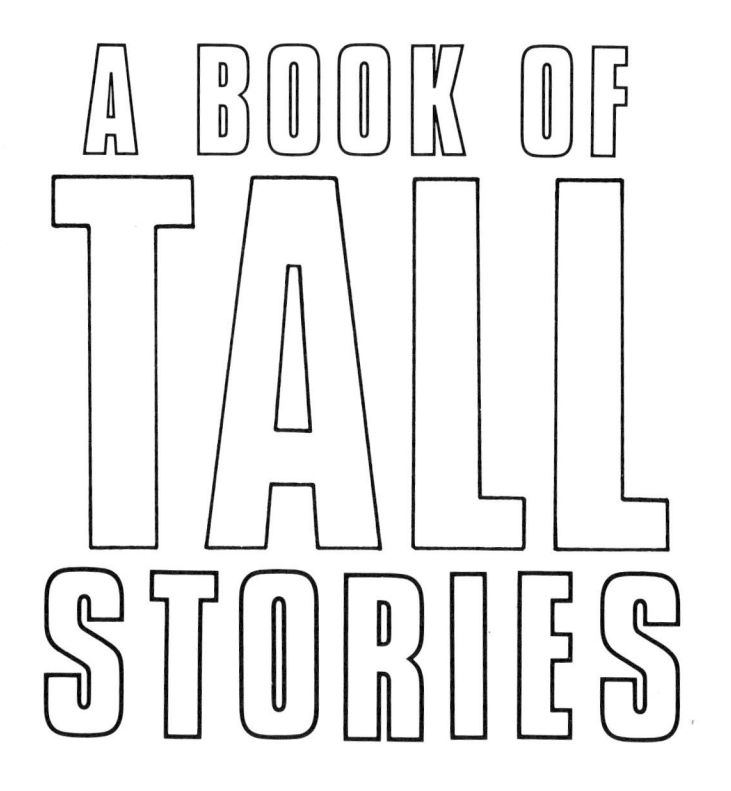

Dennis Pepper

*Dennis Pepper
(Pearse House 1989).*

Illustrations by
Allan Curless, Penny Dann, Alastair Graham,
Mark Hackett, and Nick Harris.
Cover illustration is by Alastair Graham.

Oxford University Press
Oxford   Toronto   Melbourne

Oxford University Press, Walton Street, Oxford OX2 6DP
Oxford New York Toronto
Delhi Bombay Calcutta Madras Karachi
Petaling Jaya Singapore Hong Kong Tokyo
Nairobi Dar es Salaam Cape Town
Melbourne Auckland

and associated companies in
Beirut Berlin Ibadan Nicosia

Oxford is a trade mark of Oxford University Press

© This selection and arrangement, Dennis Pepper 1987

ISBN 0 19 278101 4

All rights reserved. No part of this publication may be reproduced, stored in a retrieval system, or transmitted, in any form or by any means, electronic, mechanical, photocopying, recording, or otherwise, without the prior permission of Oxford University Press

This book is sold subject to the condition that it shall not, by way of trade or otherwise, be lent, re-sold, hired out or otherwise circulated without the publisher's prior consent in any form of binding or cover other than that in which it is published and without a similar condition including this condition being imposed on the subsequent purchaser

British Library Cataloguing in Publication Data
Pepper, Dennis
A book of tall stories.
I. Title
823'.914[J]   PZ7

ISBN 0-19-278101-4

Typeset by Oxford Publishing Services, Oxford.
Printed by Butler & Tanner Ltd, Frome

This book would have been a lot taller, but there is a shortage of tall trees, at the moment, to make tall paper . . .

Contents

I
(pages 7–21)

About what happened when Thomis was a nuisance in class and about when the whole class misbehaved; about Jenny, who bit her ear, and Rachel, who was heart-broken when her pet tortoise died; about Gretel, brought to trial for murdering a lonely old lady in a house in the woods; and about Albert, who wasn't afraid of lions

II
(pages 22–29)

About what happens when Martin comes; about the well-kept secret of the yellow ribbon; about four brothers who had the misfortune to be hunchbacked; about an unusual family pet; and about a very helpful undertaker

III
(pages 30–39)

About Captain John Santos, who had his leg chewed off by a shark and couldn't manage without his wooden one; about the girl Raymond met when he was going home on his motor-bike in the rain late one night; about what happened to the twins and to the man who jumped; and about a rare kind of seaweed

IV
(pages 40–53)

About Joe, the motor mechanic who specialized in repairing clutches, Murgatroyd the kluge-maker (first class), and Bert Williams who, as a boy, caught fish to sell to the white folks who lived up the mountain; about the rivalry between Billie the Dolphin and Eddie the Human Seal; and about a Yankee painter whose painting of a wild bear ran off in the rain

V
(pages 54–67)

About Lizzie's lion catching a rotten robber and León catching a man-eating lion; about a pet rattlesnake, the Londoners who bought a mare's egg and the man who bought a horse with most peculiar habits; about a cat with a wooden leg and the death by drowning of a tame trout; and about what happened when Pablo Romero roped a ferocious bear

VI
(pages 68–74)

About the poor man from Kasrilevka who sold Baron Rothschild the secret of eternal life and a rich man who didn't want to waste time; about a very special cake shaped like the letter S; about the gift of a lobster and about the Patcham Treacle Mines

VII
(pages 75–87)

About a helpful cow and a horse who played cricket; about a mouse who worked out how to deal with cats; about a dog who made a silly mistake but was smart enough to know what to do about it; and about John, who couldn't keep his mouth shut

VIII
(pages 88–101)

About what happened when a little old lady (and her rocking chair) went by sailing ship to Alaska; about Jonah's experiences inside the whale; about the cowboy who went to London for Queen Victoria's Jubilee; and about Morris, who knew everyone; about Okra's bad news; and what a Chinaman would do with a big, soft noodle six feet long

IX
(pages 102–111)

About what happens when the Devil challenges Jack to a trial of strength and about Jim Buckey, strong man from Montana; about the fast workers of the Australian outback and Crooked Mick, who couldn't get a job on the Speewah Station; and about the Sissy from Anaconda

X
(pages 112–119)

About hot spells in Jamaica and in the Southern States of America, the Year of the Big Freeze along the Rogue River, and being snowed up and short of fuel on Pine Mountain in Eastern Kentucky

XI
(pages 120–127)

About two remarkable hunters; about how to deal with a ferocious cougar when you've left your gun behind; and about coming upon a fourteen foot snake in Australia

XII
(pages 128–138)

About Sidehill Dodgers, Goofus Birds, Hoop Snakes and other fearsome critters; about a very nasty snake bite, cockatoos, and how to catch fur trout; about bigger and even bigger mosquitoes and a huge wolf; and about the wonderful ointment Doc Goodfellow made

XIII
(pages 139–153)

About Skunk Oil's pumpkins; Paul Bunyan's cornstalk and the crookest raffle ever run in Australia; and about Uncle Jasper's bet

Some Notes and Acknowledgements

And a narrow escape — nearly
(page 160)

Tall?
Why, they're so tall you have to stand on your shoulders just to read the page numbers.

I

The Wheelbarrow Boy 7
The Lesson 12
The Tortoise 14
The Bite 16
The Gingerbread House Caper 17
The Lion and Albert 20

The Wheelbarrow Boy

'Now see here, Thomis,' I said. 'I've just about had enough of you. If you haven't settled yourself down and started some work in two minutes' time I shall turn you into a wheelbarrow. I'm not warning you again.'

Of course, Thomis was not the only one: the whole class had the fidgets: he just happened to be the one I picked on. It was a windy day, and wind always upsets kids and makes them harder to handle. Also, I happened to know that Thomis's father had won a bit of money on the Pools, so it was easy to understand the boy's being off balance. But it's fatal to start making allowances for bad behaviour.

After about three minutes I called out, 'Well, Thomis? How many sums have you done?'

'I'm just writing the date,' said the boy sullenly.

'Right,' I said. 'You can't say I didn't warn you.' And I changed him into a wheelbarrow there and then—a bright red metal wheelbarrow with a pneumatic tyre.

The class went suddenly quiet, the way they do when you take a strong line, and during the next half-hour we got a lot of work done. When the bell for morning break went I drove them all out so as to have the room to myself.

'All right, Thomis,' I said. 'You can change back now.'

Nothing happened.

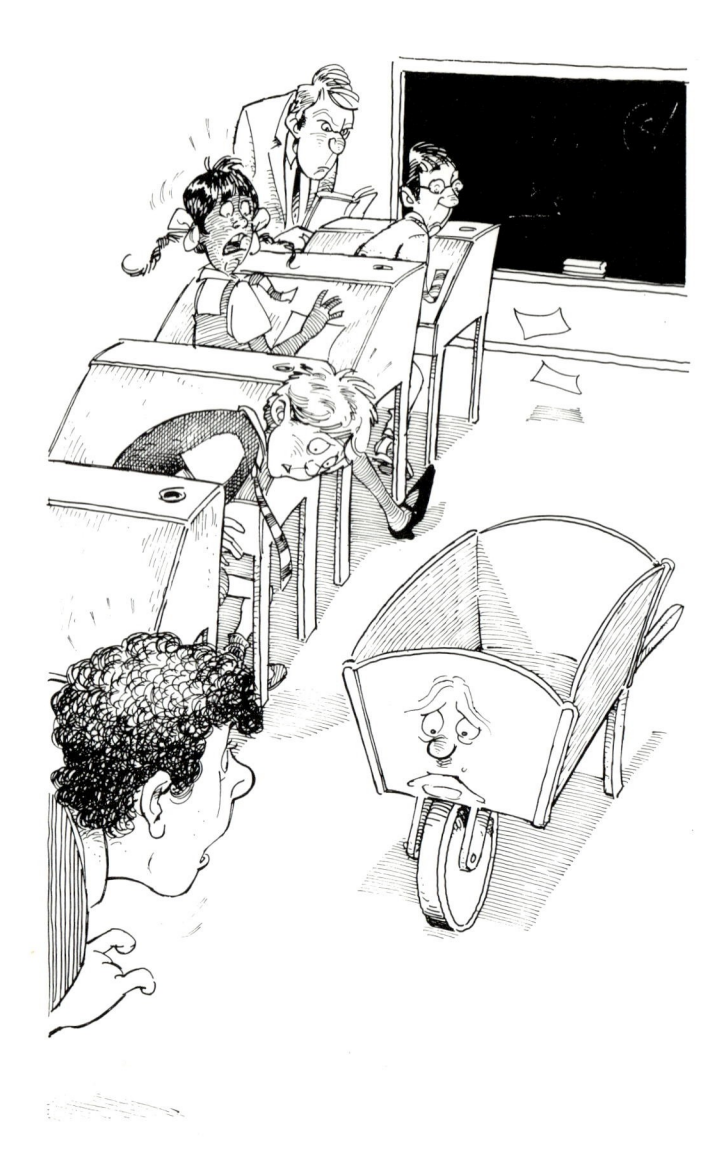

I thought at first he was sulking, but after a while I began to think that something had gone seriously wrong. I went round to the Headmaster's office.

'Look,' I said, 'I just changed Thomis into a wheelbarrow and I can't get him back.'

'Oh,' said the Head and stared at the scattering of paper on his desk. 'Are you in a violent hurry about it?'

'No,' I said. 'It's a bit worrying, though.'

'Which is Thomis?'

'Scruffy little fellow—pasty-faced—always got a sniff and a mouthful of gum.'

'Red hair?'

'No, that's Sanderson. Black, and like a bird's nest.'

'Oh yes. I've got him. Well, now,' he looked at the clock. 'Suppose you bring this Thomis chap along here in about half an hour?'

'All right,' I said.

I was a bit thoughtful as I went upstairs to the Staff Room. Tongelow was brewing the tea, and as I looked at him I remembered that he had some sort of official position in the Union.

'How would it be if I paid my Union sub?' I said.

He put the teapot down gently. 'What've you done?' he asked. 'Pushed a kid out of second-floor window?'

I pretended to be hurt. 'I just thought it was about time I paid,' I said. 'It doesn't do to get too much in arrears.'

In the end he took the money and gave me a receipt, and when I had tucked that away in my wallet I felt a lot better.

Back in my own room Thomis was still leaning up in his chair, red and awkward, a constant reproach to me. I could not start any serious work, so after about ten minutes I set the class something to keep them busy and then lifted Thomis down and wheeled him round to the Head.

'Oh, good,' he said. 'So the gardening requisition has started to come in at last.'

'No,' I said, dumping the barrow down in the middle of his carpet. 'This is Thomis. I told you . . .'

'Sorry,' he said. 'I'd clean forgotten. Leave him there and I'll get to work on him straight away. I'll send him back to you when he's presentable.'

I went back to my class and did a double period of composition, but no Thomis turned up. I thought the Old Man must have forgotten again, so when the bell went at twelve I took a peep into his room to jog his memory. He was on his knees on the carpet, jacket and tie off, with sweat pouring off his face. He got up weakly when he saw me.

'I've tried everything,' he said, 'and I can't budge him. Did you do anything unorthdox?'

'No,' I said. 'It was only a routine punishment.'

'I think you'd better ring the Union,' he said. 'Ask for Legal Aid—Maxstein's the lawyer—and see where you stand.'

'Do you mean we're stuck with this?' I said.

'You are,' said the Head. 'I should ring now, before they go to lunch.'

I got through to the Union in about ten minutes and luckily Maxstein was still there. He listened to my story, grunting now and then.

'You are a member, I suppose?'

'Oh yes,' I said.

'Paid up?'

'Certainly.'

'Good,' he said. 'Now let me see. I think I'd better ring you back in an hour or so. I've not had a case quite like this before, so I'll need to think about it.'

'Can't you give me a rough idea of how I stand?' I said.

'We're right behind you, of course,' said Maxstein. 'Free legal aid and all the rest of it. But . . . but I don't fancy your chances,' he said and rang off.

The afternoon dragged on, but there was no phone call from Maxstein. The Head got fed up with Thomis and had him wheeled out into the passage. At breaktime I phoned the Union again.

'Sorry I didn't ring you,' said Maxstein when I got through to him again. 'I've been very busy.'

'What am I to do?' I asked.

'The whole thing,' said Maxstein, 'turns on the attitude of the parents. If they decide to prosecute I'll have to come down and work out some line of defence with you.'

'Meanwhile,' I said, 'Thomis is still a wheelbarrow.'

'Quite. Now here's what I suggest. Take him home tonight—yourself. See his people and try to get some idea of their attitude. You never know; they might be grateful.'

'Grateful?' I said.

'Well, there was that case in Glasgow—kid turned into a mincing machine—and the mother was as pleased as could be and refused to have him changed back. So go round and see, and let me know in the morning.'

'All right,' I said.

At 4 o'clock I waited behind and then, when the place was empty, wheeled Thomis out into the street.

I attracted quite a lot of attention on the way, from which I guessed the story must have preceded me. A lot of people I did not know nodded or said, 'Good evening,' and three or four ran out of shops to stare.

At last I reached the place and Mr Thomis opened the door. The house seemed to be full of people and noise, so I gathered it was a party in celebration of the Pools.

He stared at me in a glazed sort of way for a moment and then made a violent effort to concentrate.

'It's Teddy's teacher,' he bawled to those inside. 'You're just in time. Come in and have a spot of something.'

'Well, actually,' I said, 'I've come about Teddy . . .'

'It can wait,' said Mr Thomis. 'Come on in.'

'No, but it's serious,' I said. 'You see, I turned Teddy into a wheelbarrow this morning, and now . . .'

'Come and have a drink first,' he said urgently.

So I went in, and drank to the healths of Mr and Mrs Thomis. 'How much did you win?' I asked politely.

'Eleven thousand quid,' said Mr Thomis. 'What a lark, eh?'

'And now,' I said firmly, 'about Teddy.'

'Oh, this weelbarrow caper,' said Mr Thomis. 'We'll soon see about that.'

He dragged me outside into the yard and went up to the wheelbarrow. 'Is this him?' he said.

I nodded.

'Now look here, Teddy,' said Mr Thomis fiercely. 'Just you come to your senses this minute, or I'll bash the daylights out of you.' And as he spoke he began to unbuckle a heavy belt that was playing second fiddle to his braces.

The wheelbarrow changed back into Teddy Thomis and nipped smartly down the garden and through a hole in the fence.

'There you are,' said Mr Thomis. 'Trouble with you teachers is you're too soft with the kids. Here, come in and have another drink.'

The Lesson

A poem that raises the question:
Should there be capital punishment in schools?

Chaos ruled OK in the classroom
as bravely the teacher walked in
the nooligans ignored him
his voice was lost in the din

'The theme for today is violence
and homework will be set
I'm going to teach you a lesson
one that you'll never forget'

He picked on a boy who was shouting
and throttled him then and there
then garrotted the girl behind him
(the one with grotty hair)

Then sword in hand he hacked his way
between the chattering rows
'First come, first severed' he declared
'fingers, feet, or toes'

He threw the sword at a latecomer
it struck with deadly aim
then pulling out a shotgun
he continued with his game

The first blast cleared the backrow
(where those who skive hang out)
they collapsed like rubber dinghies
when the plug's pulled out

'Please may I leave the room sir?'
a trembling vandal enquired
'Of course you may' said teacher
put the gun to this temple and fired

The Head popped a head round the doorway
to see why a din was being made
nodded understandingly
then tossed in a grenade

And when the ammo was well spent
with blood on every chair
Silence shuffled forward
with its hands up in the air

The teacher surveyed the carnage
the dying and the dead
He waggled a finger severely
'Now let that be a lesson' he said

> Constable John Knight told the court that on 30 June David Durbin had said to him: 'I'll kill you.'
> 'Did he kill you?' asked the prosecutor, Mr H A Kelly.

The Tortoise

'What's the matter with her?' asked Ben when he came home from work to find that his small daughter had locked herself in her bedroom.

'It's Norton,' Jill said.

'Norton?'

'The tortoise. It's died and Rachel's been crying her eyes out all day. Won't eat, won't come out, won't even talk to me now. Just what I'm supposed to do about it I really don't know.'

After half an hour sitting uncomfortably at the top of the stairs, Ben finally persuaded Rachel to open her door. He sat her on his knee and talked to her about Norton.

Yes, Norton had been a wonderful pet.

Did she remember how Norton had let her dress him in dolly clothes and push him around in her dolly pram?

Hadn't Norton always followed her about the garden chomping up the dandelions when she pointed them out to him?

And, yes, it was very, very sad but the thing now was to do what Norton would have wanted to show him how much she loved him.

'Do you remember,' said Ben, 'how he used to bury himself in the garden every year when the cold weather came? What do we call it?'

'Hiberrate.'

'Hibernate, yes. Norton loved to hibernate. So what do you say if we get a box from Mummy and make Norton all cosy in it with straw and cotton wool?'

'I don't know.'

'And you can put some special presents in it for him and some of his favourite food. Grapes. He liked grapes, didn't he?'

'Yes.'

'We'll dig a special place for him under the roses and you can make a cross with his name on. Then when we've put him in you can find some really pretty stones and make a circle all round where he is. You would like that, wouldn't you?'

'Yes.'

'And just so we never forget what a very special tortoise Norton was we'll ask Mummy for a jar to put next to the cross. You can put fresh flowers in it every day.'

'And take Teddy with me to see him?'

'And take Teddy with you to see him.'

And so Rachel put away her tears and came downstairs to have some tea. While she was telling Jill what a wonderful funeral they were going to give Norton and how she was going to sing hymns and take flowers to him every morning, Ben went out to get a fork from the shed. There he found Norton on his back, legs in the air. When Ben turned him right way up he sighed, hicupped, and went off to eat the lettuces. So all was well. Ben hadn't been too keen on starting an animal cemetery in the back garden and now Rachel had her precious Norton back. With luck he could live for fifty years. He went inside with the good news.

'Oh!' said Rachel. Pause. 'Let's kill him.'

The Bite

Jenny entered the Medical Room with her hand pressed against the side of her head.

'Name?' said the nurse, not looking up from her desk.

'Jenny Smith, Miss.'

'Form?'

'4RW, Miss.'

'Note.'

'I haven't got one, Miss.'

Nurse looked up. 'Haven't got one!'

'No, Miss.'

'Then take your hand away! Come along, girl, let me have a look.'

'I've bit my ear, Miss.'

'Bit your ear! Don't be silly. How on earth can you bite your own ear?'

'I stood on a chair, Miss.'

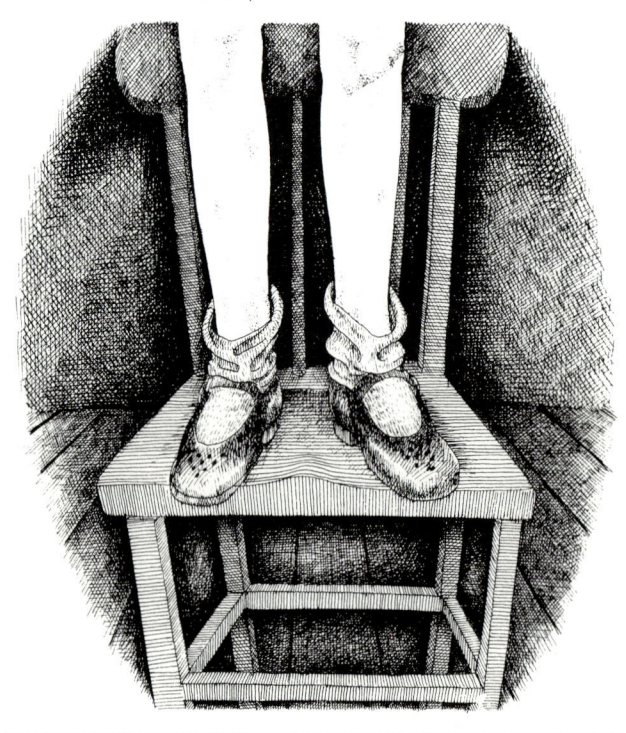

'My brother's so tall he has to climb a ladder to comb his hair.'
'*My* brother's feet are so big he has to go outside to turn round.'

16

The Gingerbread House Caper

You all remember Hansel and Gretel, with their story about the gingerbread house and the witch. Imagine what a good District Attorney could do with that tale today.

'You do admit,' he says to Gretel before a hushed courtroom, 'that you tricked the little old lady into climbing into the oven and then slamming the door.'

'But she was going to bake us,' says Gretel.

'Did she *say* she was going to bake you?'

'No, she said she was going to bake bread.'

'And she had, in fact, already kneaded the dough. Yet you somehow knew she was going to bake you instead.'

'I could tell,' Gretel says. 'Women can sense these things.'

'I see. Now you also say she kept Hansel locked up in a stable for four weeks, in order to fatten him up. Yet her eyesight was so bad that every morning when she went to feel his finger, he easily fooled her by holding out a small bone instead. I ask the jury to bear that in mind. Now, will you please describe your actions after releasing your brother.'

'We went home.'

'Yes, we know, but I think the record will show that you didn't go straight home. Tell us, please, what you did first?'

'We fell on each other's neck.'

'And?'

'Danced about . . . and kissed.'

'Go on.'

'Oh, just picked up some pearls and precious stones that we found around the house.'

'Well, well. It seems the little old lady wasn't the only one who "needed dough". Now, when you first saw that house, you started eating it. Didn't it occur to you that it might belong to somebody?'

'I guess we didn't think.'

'You didn't think. Well, I suggest you thought about it very carefully. That this was a well-planned, well-executed operation. Pretending to be lost, you gained entrance to the home of a half-blind old lady, lulled her into a false sense of security and with premeditation, disposed of her in the grisly manner described.'

'No! It wasn't like that!'

'Now you state that on your way home, you crossed a large body of water—on a duck, if you please. If there were such a body of water, why didn't you cross it on the *way* to the gingerbread house? I'll tell you why. You returned in a round-about way to cover your tracks.'

'We were lost.' Gretel is sniffling now. 'We were just a couple of little kids.'

'And you arrived home to find your stepmother conveniently dead. I'm curious as to how you arranged that.'

'We didn't have anything to do with that.'

'But you *did* hate her. Because you felt that she rejected you. She got your father to abandon you in the woods. Clearly a form of rejection. And anyone who crosses you is in for a rough time. She found that out, and so did the old lady.'

'She was no old lady! She was a witch!'

'Now, suppose we go back a bit. Why didn't you release your brother and make good your escape at the very beginning of your so-called captivity?'

'I was afraid the witch would catch us and bring us back.'

'You thought a lame, weak-eyed old woman could catch two lively children in the middle of the woods?'

'It's the truth, the truth!'

'And I submit that you didn't escape because that would have spoiled your plans. You were willing to wait four weeks for the chance to shove her into the oven and make off with the jewels.'

'But I never even noticed them before.'

'A chestful of them in every corner of the house and you never noticed them. You expect us to believe that?'

Gretel shakes her head, sobbing now.

'Ladies and gentlemen of the jury,' the District Attorney says. 'Consider this sweet-looking child, with the apron and the wooden shoes and the crocodile tears. Now visualize this same girl and her brother, rejoicing, dancing, kissing, even as the kindly old lady is roasting away. Does this picture suggest a couple of mistreated innocents — or rather a pair of calloused conspirators who have just pulled off the crime of the century? I have no further questions.'

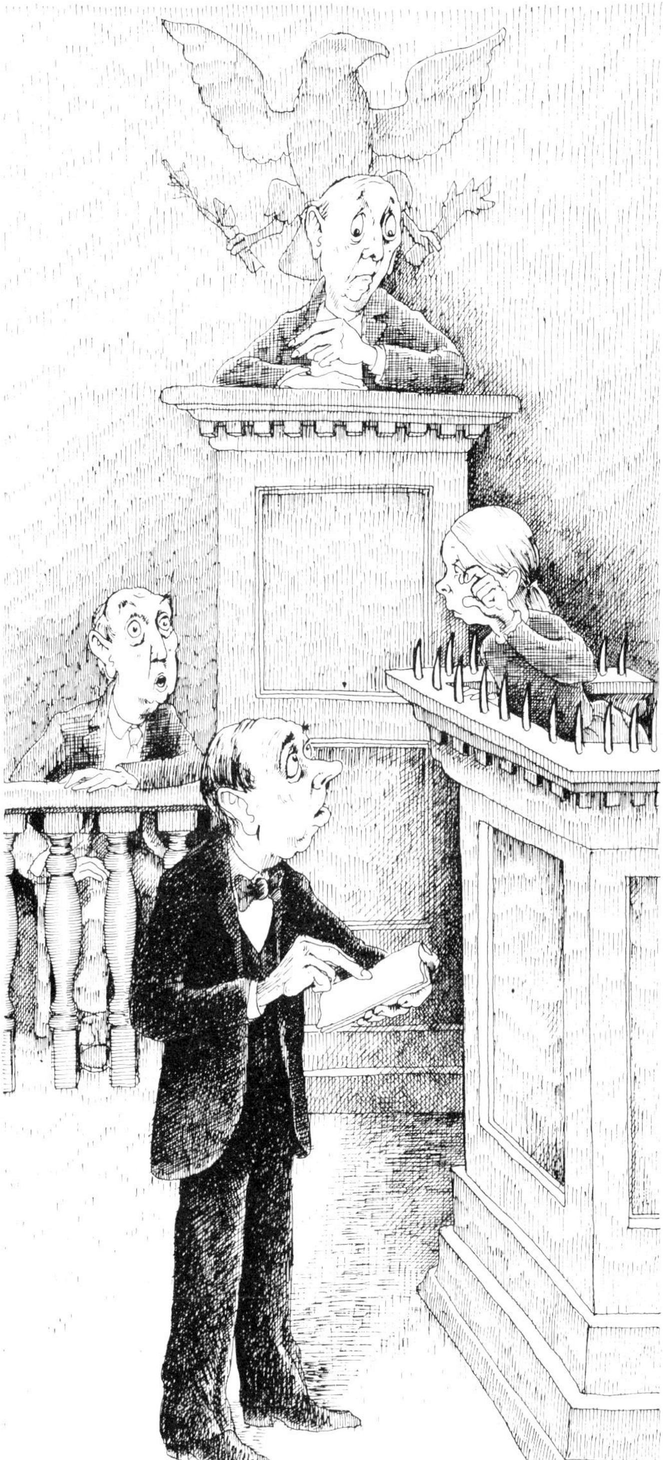

The Lion and Albert

There's a famous seaside place called Blackpool,
    That's noted for fresh air and fun,
And Mr and Mrs Ramsbottom
    Went there with young Albert, their son.

A grand little lad was young Albert,
    All dressed in his best; quite a swell
With a stick with an 'orse's 'ead 'andle,
    The finest that Woolworth's could sell.

They didn't think much to the Ocean:
    The waves, they was fiddlin' and small,
There was no wrecks and nobody drownded,
    Fact, nothing to laugh at at all.

So, seeking for further amusement,
    They paid and went into the Zoo,
Where they'd Lions and Tigers and Camels,
    And old ale and sandwiches too.

There were one great big Lion called Wallace;
    His nose were all covered with scars —
He lay in a somnolent posture
    With the side of his face on the bars.

Now Albert had heard about Lions,
    How they was ferocious and wild —
To see Wallace lying so peaceful,
    Well, it didn't seem right to the child.

So straightway the brave little feller,
    Not showing a morsel of fear,
Took his stick with its 'orse's 'ead 'andle
    And poked it in Wallace's ear.

You could see that the Lion didn't like it,
    For giving a kind of a roll,
He pulled Albert inside the cage with 'im,
    And swallowed the little lad 'ole.

Then Pa, who had seen the occurrence,
    And didn't know what to do next,
Said 'Mother! Yon Lion's 'et Albert,'
    And Mother said 'Well, I am vexed!'

Then Mr and Mrs Ramsbottom —
    Quite rightly, when all's said and done —
Complained to the Animal Keeper
    That the Lion had eaten their son.

The keeper was quite nice about it;
    He said 'What a nasty mishap.
Are you sure that it's *your* boy he's eaten?'
    Pa said 'Am I sure? There's his cap!'

The manager had to be sent for.
    He came and he said 'What's to do?'
Pa said 'Yon Lion's 'et Albert,
    And 'im in his Sunday clothes, too.'

Then Mother said, 'Right's right, young feller;
    I think it's a shame and a sin
For a lion to go and eat Albert,
    And after we've paid to come in.'

The manager wanted no trouble,
    He took out his purse right away,
Saying 'How much to settle the matter?'
    And Pa said 'What do you usually pay?'

But Mother had turned a bit awkward
    When she thought where her Albert had gone.
She said 'No! someone's got to be summonsed' —
    So that was decided upon.

Then off they went to the P'lice Station,
    In front of the Magistrate chap;
They told 'im what happened to Albert,
    And proved it by showing his cap.

The Magistrate gave his opinion
    That no one was really to blame
And he said that he hoped the Ramsbottoms
    Would have further sons to their name.

At that Mother got proper blazing,
    'And thank you, sir, kindly,' said she.
'What, waste all our lives raising children
    To feed ruddy Lions? Not me!'

II

Wait Till Martin Comes 22
The Yellow Ribbon 24
The Four Hunchbacks 26
A Family Pet 28
The Helpful Undertaker 29

Wait Till Martin Comes

There was no doubt about it, he was lost. He knew he could get back to some kind of road just by going downhill but the trees were getting thicker and night was drawing in. He was just making up his mind to spend the night in the open when he came to a big abandoned house, standing all by itself in the middle of the woods. The door was open and he went in. There was nobody there, and no furniture in most of the rooms; but in one room there was a big old-fashioned bed, standing by itself in the middle of the floor. This was real luck; he cut some wood and made a fire on the hearth, ate what food he had, and stretched out on the bed.

The fire was burning low, and he was getting sleepy when a little kitten came in, walked three times round the bed, spat in the fire, and sat down on the hearth and looked at him. He was just thinking what a cute kitten it was, when a big tomcat came in, walked three times round the bed, spat in the fire, and sat down on the hearth by the kitten, and they both looked at him. Then the kitten said, 'Shall we do it now?' And the tomcat said, 'No, we got to wait till Martin comes.'

The boy was scared, of course, but before he could make up his mind whether to run, a big bobcat came in, walked three times round the bed, spat in the fire, and sat on the hearth and looked at him. Then the kitten and the tomcat turned to the bobcat and said, 'Shall we do it now?' And the bobcat said, 'No, we got to wait till Martin comes.'

By this time the boy was so scared he could hardly move, and it seemed better to lie perfectly still anyway. Then a mountain lion came in, walked three times round the bed, spat in the fire, which was almost out, and sat on the hearth and looked at him. And the other three turned to the mountain lion and said, 'Shall we do it now?' And the mountain lion said, 'No, we got to wait till Martin comes.'

Then a huge Bengal tiger came in, padded three times round the bed, and spat in the fire and put out the last spark, and sat on the hearth and looked at him. It was pitch-dark without the fire, but he could see the five pairs of green eyes looking at him. And four of them said to the tiger, 'Shall we do it *now*?' And the tiger said, 'No, we can't do nothing till Martin comes—*and Martin*—AIN'T COMING!'

And they all walked out.

The Yellow Ribbon

Janet and John did everything together. They played together, went on holiday together, got in trouble together and, when they were five, went to school together. They were in the same class and sat at the same table.

One day John said, 'Why do you always wear a yellow ribbon round your neck?'

'I can't tell you,' said Janet.

'Why not?'

'I just can't, that's all.'

John kept asking, so at last Janet said she would tell him later — perhaps.

But she didn't. From time to time John would remember. 'Hey!' he would say, 'what about your ribbon? You promised to tell me why you wear it.'

'No, I didn't.'

'Yes, you did.'

'I didn't. I said "maybe".'

Whenever John asked, Janet would find some way to get out of telling him.

They went on to the big school, studied the same subjects, took the same examinations. On their last day at school, John asked again.

'No,' said Janet, 'not today. It would spoil things.'

'When, then?'

'Oh, some day.'

They left school, went out together, got engaged.

'Well, at least now you can tell me about your ribbon,' said John, reaching towards it.

'Oh, no!' said Janet, moving quickly away. She made him promise he would never try to take her ribbon off unless she said he could. On their wedding day — perhaps — she would tell him.

But John forgot to ask and Janet didn't remind him. After, when he remembered, Janet just shook her head and smiled sweetly.

'We're happy, aren't we?' she said. 'There's nothing wrong between us. We'll have a lovely life together. What difference does it make?'

It didn't make any difference and they had a lovely life together.

Many years later, when even their grandchildren had grown up and married, Janet fell seriously ill. It soon became clear that she was dying. Each day, for many hours, John sat by her bed telling over for her all the happy things with which their lives together had been filled.

'Do you remember,' he said one day, 'how I used to tease you about your yellow ribbon?'

'Indeed I do,' said Janet. 'I suppose you can untie it now.'

So John untied the yellow ribbon, and Janet's head fell off.

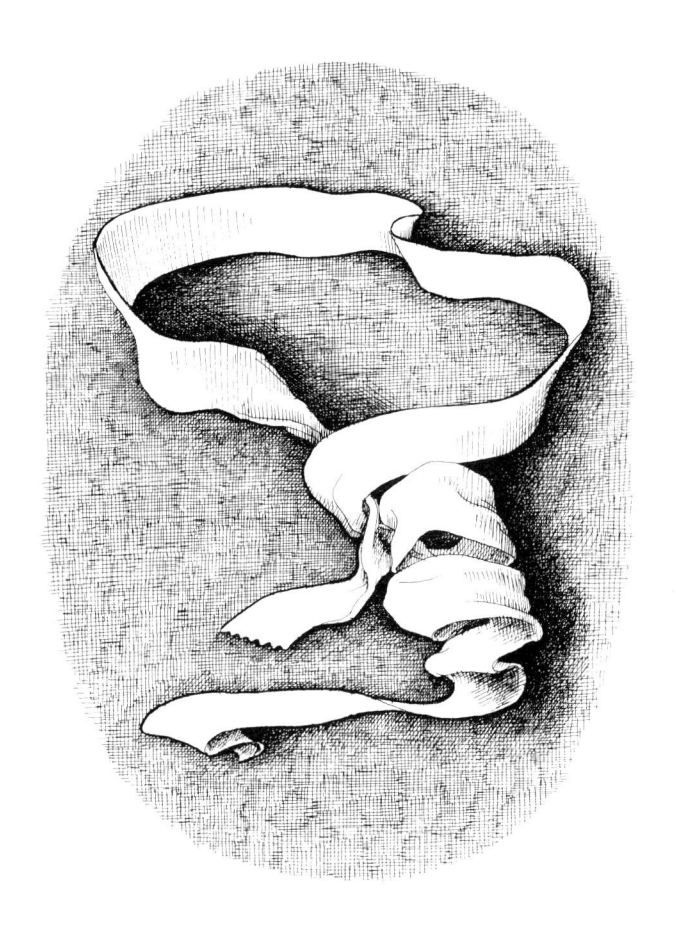

The Four Hunchbacks

Three hunchbacked brothers lived with their father in a village in the deep woods. They were all woodcutters. One day the father, who was an old man, died. When he had been buried, the brothers said to each other, 'There is no need for us to stay any longer in the woods. Let us go to our brother in the city.'

So they dressed in their best clothes and went to the city. They found the shop which their brother owned, and they entered. Their brother, also a hunchback, was not there, but his wife was tending the shop. When they told her who they were, her heart sank. She said to herself, 'Now my husband will want to take care of these hillbillies. We'll have to share everything with them!' But she talked nicely as though they were welcome, and she took them to her house and fed them; but she put poison into their food so that they died.

Then she found a man with a boat, and she told him she'd give him twenty-five dollars if he'd take a body out to sea and dispose of it. So he came to the house, and she showed him one of the bodies. He put it in a sack and carried it down to his boat. He took the body out to sea and threw it overboard. Then he came back for his money. She then showed him the body of the second brother and said, 'But you haven't done the work yet. Here is the body just where I left it.' The boatman was confused. He was sure he had already done the job. But he put the second body in his sack, lugged it to his boat, and went out to sea with it.

He returned after that to the woman's house, but she said, 'What kind of a man are you that wants to be paid before he works?' And she showed him the body of the third brother. The boatman became furious. 'So you've come back!' he shouted at the body. 'This time you are going out to sea to stay!' And he carted the body down to his boat. This time he sailed far out to sea and disposed of it. 'That is the end,' the boatman said. 'Now I will get my money.'

He returned to the woman's house. Night was just falling, and the woman's husband was just returning. When the boatman's eyes fell on him he went into a rage.

'So!' he shouted, 'So you're back again! And walking around, too! I'll fix you this time.' He leaped upon the woman's husband and killed him, dragged his body down to the sea, and threw it in.

> **She's so mean she'd steal a fly from a blind spider.**

A Family Pet

Acme Sulphide came in from his prospect on Caribou creek, bringing a big cougar to Larry Frazee's taxidermist shop. 'Want him skun out and made into a rug?' asked Larry.

'No sir. Stuff him as is. I wouldn't think of walkun on Petronius.'

'Why not? Just a cougar, ain't he?'

'Not by your tin horn. He's an institution, that's what he is. When he was just a kitten I ketched him by the mine shaft. Him and Pluto, they was great friends until Petronius growed up. Then one evening when I comes back, my Pluto was gone and Petronius wouldn't eat his supper. I was plumb mad, but I figgered Pluto was gettun old and wasn't so much account nohow. Then, by gum, I missed Mary, the goat. When I missed the last of the chickens and Petronius showed up with feathers in his whiskers, I made up my mind to shoot him. But I got to thinkun how that goat could butt, and the hens wasn't layun anyhow. So I let it go. But I shoulda bumped him then.

'Lydie, she's my old woman—or she was. Partner of my joys and sorrows for forty years. One evening when I gets back she was gone. No sign of her anywhere exceptun one shoe. And Petronius didn't want no supper again. That got me mad, danged if it didn't, and I went for my gun to blast the varmint. Then I got to thinkun. Lydie wasn't much for looks and besides, she was about to leave me. She was all for hittun the trail, so I puts my gun up.'

'Then what happened?'

'Well, last night he jumped me on the trail and took a big hunk right out of me. That was too danged much. So mount him up pretty. He repersents my whole family.'

The Helpful Undertaker

She went to the Undertaker's to see the body of her husband as he lay in the Chapel of Rest.

'Oh, you've made him look really nice!' she said, then hesitated a moment. 'There is one thing, though.'

'Please, madam, if we can be of any help . . .?' The undertaker paused.

'Well, you see, I know I said I would like him to be in a brown suit but I rather think now that grey would have been better. He always looked good in grey. More distinguished, if you know what I mean.'

'I do indeed, madam. If you prefer grey of course, we can easily make the change. I'm sure it wouldn't do if he were to feel at all uncomfortable once he has passed over.'

When she saw her husband the next day she was well satisfied. 'So very much better,' she said. 'So very much more suitable. I'm only sorry I put you to such trouble.'

'Oh, no trouble, madam, no trouble at all. As it happened we had a gentleman with us dressed in grey and as his good lady said she would really have preferred brown we made the exchange. Quite convenient, as you might say.'

'You are very kind. Whatever you say, I'm sure it must have been very difficult changing all those clothes.'

'Oh, no, madam,' said the undertaker. 'We just changed the heads!'

III

Cap'n Santos' Leg   30
Raymond and Nellie   32
The Twins   35
Framed in a First-storey Winder . . .   36
The Telltale Seaweed   37

Cap'n Santos' Leg

'You fellers wouldn't remember old Cap'n John Santos—feller that had his leg et off by a shark on the Western Banks. But I can remember him, back when I was a boy, and how proud he was of the new juryleg they rigged him up with. It was a sight, I tell you, to watch him dance a jig with that leg and not nick the floor once. Carried around furniture polish just like the doctor carries iodine, in case of a cut or scratch, and one time he copper-bottomed her to make sure the worms wouldn't get to him before his time.

'Well, you know once a man is chawed on by a shark, he's shark-jonahed for the rest of his life. Some day a shark's going to get the rest of that feller, if he keeps on going to sea. And Cap'n John kept on.

'The Cap'n's trawler, the *Hetty K*, was ten mile from the Race when the Portland Gale struck. That was November 27. On the 28th she come crippling round the Point under bare poles with two foot of harbour water over her lee rail. The crew said Cap'n John was washed overboard, along with two other men.

'The bodies of the other two drifted ashore; the Cap'n wasn't never found. But a couple of days after, Joe Barcia picked up the old man's wooden leg off the beach. He took it home to Mary Santos, the widow.

'Married thirty years, them two. When Joe Barcia brought back the leg, Mary took it into the house. She petted it and talked to it.

'Nothing more come of it till the night of November 26, a year later. That night, Mary said, she set up in bed, and there, standing straight as two yards of pump-water on his one leg, was old Cap'n John. He hopped over alongside the bed and canted over. Then he whispered to her.

' "Barometer's falling, Mary," he says, "and the wind's no'th east. We're in for thick weather, and I'll want my store leg to keep me steady when she strikes." He pinched her cheek, and Mary let out a yell. When she looked again, the Cap'n was gone.

'Next morning, Mary said, she had a little red spot on her cheek. And before she turned in that night, she took the skipper's leg out of the spice-cupboard and left it laid out for him in a corner near the fireplace.

'That night a breeze of wind come up, and in a couple of hours it turned into a living gale—from the no'th east. The willer tree outside howled like the yo-ho bird of every dead sailor in hell come there to roost. All of a sudden Mary hears a thump-thump-thump across the floor, down below, and then the door shut to. She stayed in bed.

'Next morning she went to look if the Cap'n's leg was still there. It was, but when she picked it up, it was wet.

'Well, it'd rained bad enough to come in by the chimney. But it gallied her so, the sight of the that leg with the water on it, that she got sick. She called in Doc Atwood. When he got through sounding, and didn't find nothing sprung, Doc said something was eating on her. Then she told him the whole story.

'When he'd went over the leg, he looked hard at the widow.

' "You say you left it by the fireplace all night and rain come in on it?" he asks. Then he sets the leg down, comes over to the widow, and tells her straight out. "Mrs Santos," he says, "I'm going to ask you to have one of the men take this thing out to sea, and weight it with netleads, and heave it overboard. I'm a doctor," he says, "and I don't listen to stories. But Mrs Santos," he says, "I put my tongue to that wood. *It don't rain salt water!*" '

The wind blew every feather from a flock of Black Langshan chickens without killing one of them. Scared them, though. The feathers that grew back in were snow-white.

Raymond and Nellie

It was raining.

The motorcycle lamp poked a finger of light through the dark soaking slant of the rain as the machine spattered and hummed along the highway.

The young man, hunched miserably on it, suddenly started upright and throttled back a second later.

The beam of the headlight had picked up a bedraggled figure in white, huddling at the edge of the road.

Raymond slowed and stopped.

'Want a ride?'

The girl stood as if she had not heard, water dripping from her hair, from the indistinct chin, from the shapeless dress.

'Get on,' Raymond said.

The girl nodded as if in a trance, then slowly got up on the machine behind him. He felt her arms come around him, and her cheek touched his back. This could be very pleasant, he thought, if it were not for the rain.

'Here we go,' he said. Then he remembered that she wore only the dress. He peeled off his black leather jacket and helped her put it on. She seemed nearly helpless. He wondered if she could hold on. He felt a sudden tenderness for her and decided to go slow.

The rain drove through his shirt, but he had the good feeling that he was helping someone who needed help.

He kicked off and they splashed along the highway. They chugged over a little white bridge and went on.

It was too miserable for talk. He just hunched over, swore to himself at the rain, and hoped there was a town near. He would see her home and they could talk later.

Two or three minutes later there were the lights of the town. He pulled up carefully before a diner that looked warm, and then he got the shock of his life.

The girl was gone.

Raymond tugged the wheel around and was just

about to go. 'No, I've got to get some help,' he thought.

He ran into the diner.

'Need some help!' he said, trembling with the shock.

There was only an old man behind the counter. He wore a tall white chef's cap. 'What for?' he said.

'I picked up a girl. She—I guess she fell off. I didn't notice, the rain—'

The old man turned, picked up a pot and poured a cup of coffee. He set it down for Raymond.

'You didn't pick up no girl,' he said.

Raymond stared at him. 'She's back there! You've got to get a car—I can't bring her in. I'm riding a motor-cycle!'

'You didn't pick up no girl, son.'

Raymond groaned. He ran out and kicked the cycle into a roar and tore back on the highway. He stared at the road, dreading what he'd see. Then with a shock he realized he had passed the little white bridge.

He went a short way and stopped. He didn't know what to do.

Lights came along behind him, and the chugging sound of an old Ford. It stopped and the old fellow from the diner rolled down a window and said. 'See anything?'

Raymond shook his head.

'Follow me,' the old man said.

The Ford rolled on and Raymond, not knowing why, followed it.

It turned off almost immediately and splashed up a puddled gravel road through a grove of trees and stopped. The old man got out and walked through an archway.

Raymond followed.

The rain had stopped suddenly. Everything was cold and clear and the moon came from behind a ragged edge of cloud.

The light glanced off something, and Raymond saw that he was standing beside the old man and reading from the stone:

On the slab beneath the stone was his black leather jacket.

The Twins

In form and feature, face and limb,
    I grew so like my brother
That folks got taking me for him
    And each for one another.
It puzzled all our kith and kin,
    It reach'd an awful pitch;
For one of us was born a twin
    And not a soul knew which.

One day (to make the matter worse),
    Before our names were fix'd,
As we were being wash'd by nurse,
    We got completely mix'd.
And thus, you see, by Fate's decree,
    (Or rather nurse's whim),
My brother John got christen'd *me*,
    And I got christen'd *him*.

This fatal likeness even dogg'd
    My footsteps when at school,
And I was always getting flogg'd —
    For John turn'd out a fool.
I put this question hopelessly
    To every one I knew, —
What *would* you do, if you were me,
    To prove that you were *you*?

Our close resemblance turn'd the tide
    Of my domestic life;
For somehow my intended bride
    Became my brother's wife.
In short, year after year the same
    Absurd mistakes went on;
And when I died — the neighbours came
    And buried brother John!

The climate is so healthy in California they had to shoot a man before they could start a graveyard.

Framed in a First-storey Winder

Framed in a first-storey winder of a burnin' buildin'
Appeared: A Yuman Ead!
Jump into this net, wot we are 'oldin'
And yule be quite orl right!

But 'ee wouldn't jump . . .

And the flames grew Igher and Igher and Igher.
(Phew!)

Framed in a second-storey winder of a burnin' buildin'
Appeared: A Yuman Ead!
Jump into this net, wot we are 'oldin'
And yule be quite orl right!

But 'ee wouldn't jump . . .

And the flames grew Igher and Igher and Igher
(Strewth!)

Framed in a third-storey winder of a burnin' buildin'
Appeared: A Yuman Ead!
Jump into this net, wot we are 'oldin'
And yule be quite orl right!
Honest!

And 'ee jumped . . .

And 'ee broke 'is bloomin' neck!

Dry? A drop of water hit a feller once and they had to throw two buckets of dirt in his face to bring him round.

The Telltale Seaweed

It seems that one chilly October night in the first decade of the present century, two sisters were motoring along a Cape Cod road when their car broke down just before midnight and would go no further.

This was in an era when such mishaps were both commoner and more hopeless than they are today. For these two, there was no chance of help until another car might chance to come by in the morning and give them a tow. Of a lodging for the night there was no hope except a gaunt, unlighted frame house which stood black in the moonlight across a neglected stretch of frost-hardened lawn.

They yanked at its ancient bellpull, but only a faint tinkle within made answer. They banged despairingly on the door panel, only to awaken what at first they thought was an echo and then identified as a shutter responding antiphonally with the help of a nipping wind. This shutter was around the corner, and the ground-floor window behind it was broken and unfastened. There was enough moonlight to show that the room within was a deserted library, with a few books left on the sagging shelves and a few pieces of dilapidated furniture still standing where some departing family had left them, long before. At least the sweep of the electric flash which one of the women had brought with her showed them that on the uncarpeted floor the dust lay thick and trackless, as if no one had trod there in many a day.

They decided to bring their blankets in from the car and stretch out there on the floor until daylight—none too comfortable, perhaps, but at least sheltered from that salt and cutting wind. It was while they were lying there trying to get to sleep, while, indeed, they had drifted halfway across the borderland, that they saw—each confirming the other's fear by a convulsive grip of the hand—saw standing at the empty fireplace, as if trying to dry himself by a fire that was not there, the wraithlike figure of a sailor, come dripping from the sea.

After an endless moment, in which neither sister breathed, one of them somehow found the strength to call out, 'Who's there?' The challenge shattered the

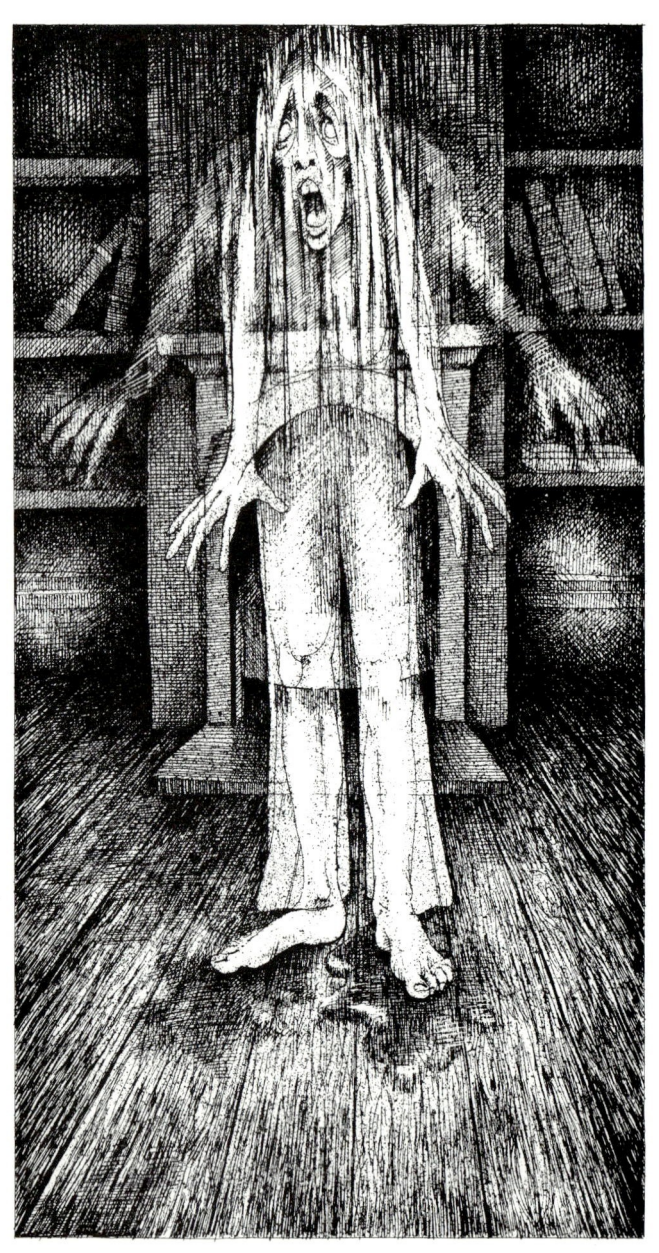

intolerable silence, and at the sound, muttering a little—they said afterwards that it was something between a groan and a whimper—the misty figure seemed to dissolve. They strained their eyes but could see nothing between themselves and the battered mantelpiece. Then telling themselves (and, as one does, half believing it) that they had been dreaming, they tried again to sleep and, indeed, did sleep until a patch of shuttered sunlight striped the morning floor. As they sat up and blinked at the gritty realism of the forsaken room, they would, I think, have laughed at their shared illusion of the night before, had it not been for something at which one of the sisters pointed with a kind of gasp. There in the still undisturbed dust, on the spot in front of the fireplace where the apparition had seemed to stand, was a patch of water—a little, circular pool that had issued from no crack in the floor nor, as far as they could see, fallen from any point in the innocent ceiling. Near it in the surrounding dust was no footprint—their own or any other's—and in it was a piece of green that looked like seaweed. One of the women bent down and put her finger to the water, then lifted it to her tongue. The water was salty.

After that the sisters scuttled out and sat in their car until a passerby gave them a tow to the nearest village. In the tavern at breakfast they gossiped with the proprietress about the empty house down the road. Oh, yes, it had been just that way for a score of years or more. Folks did say the place was spooky, haunted by a son of the family who, driven out by his father, had shipped before the mast and been drowned at sea. Some said the family had moved away because they could not stand the things they heard and saw at night.

A year later, one of the sisters told the story at a dinner party in New York. In the pause that followed a man across the table leaned forward. 'My dear lady,' he said, 'I happen to be the curator of a museum where they are doing a good deal of work on submarine vegetation. In your place, I never would have left that house without taking the bit of seaweed with me.'

'Of course you wouldn't,' she answered tartly, 'and neither did I.'

It seems she had lifted it out of the water and dried it a little by pressing it against a windowpane. Then she had carried it off in her pocketbook, as a souvenir. As far as she knew, it was still in an envelope in a little drawer of her desk at home. If she could find it, would he like to see it? He would. Next morning she sent it around by messenger, and a few days later it came back with a note.

'You were right,' the note said, 'this is seaweed. Furthermore, it may interest you to learn that it is of a rare variety which, as far as we know, grows only on dead bodies.'

IV

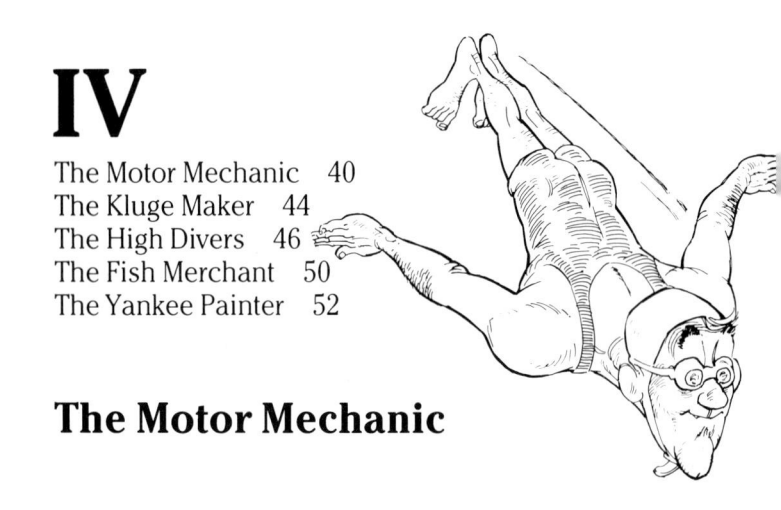

The Motor Mechanic 40
The Kluge Maker 44
The High Divers 46
The Fish Merchant 50
The Yankee Painter 52

The Motor Mechanic

The afternoon was wearing on and the streets would soon be crowded with the rush-hour ritual. Joe had given up the day when a car floundered beside him.

Joe watched it tilt crazily as the man wound up the jack.

'I'll give you a hand' he said. 'I could hold it at the other side to stop it falling over.'

The driver grunted as he heaved a spare wheel from the boot. Joe crouched his weight between the car and the road, occasionally directing passing vehicles with his free arm. When the traffic lights were at red he made sure they stopped. And when they changed to green, he encouraged them to move again. The pressure on his shoulder eased as the car bounced back on its new limb.

'Well . . . That's a good job well done,' said Joe across the bonnet.

'You still here?' said the driver.

'What would you have done without me? I threw an accordion around the place. I've been stuck here, perverting the traffic and holding up your car at the same time, and all you can say is are you still here.'

Joe stood between the driver and the door handle. The driver tried to summon the energy to argue, but it was now raining and Joe was talking.

'It's hard work you know, keeping a car this size from falling over. And as for the other cars, they'd all have run into you if it wasn't for me!'

The driver produced his wallet with a covering smile. Joe's outstretched hand was covered by a pound note and his mouth closed.

'I don't know why he's in such a hurry,' thought

Joe as the car drove off, 'it'll be just as wet where he's going! That wasn't a bad pound's worth, though.'

He considered the possibilities as he bumped along the rush-hour pavement.

'It's no' a bad job being a motor mechanic. Well paid, out in the open air . . .' A motor mechanic was a very educated sort of job, and he would have made a good one except that he knew nothing about motors. But he could find out before looking for a job in the morning. Joe spent that night with a couple of library books in front of the fire. When he became confused by one he switched to the other until it became too much. He went to bed full of mechanical knowledge.

Next morning Joe was up early and enthusiastic. He looked for a garage with a lot of cars. He found one without much trouble and went to see the boss.

The manager listened sympathetically to Joe's story about his long illness and how he had nursed his one-legged granny and carried her everywhere because someone had stolen her crutch.

'Oh yes,' said Joe tearfully, 'these were hard times. I survived it all and those who laughed are now shook with shame, for the poor old soul has gone where the lame can see.'

'Well, Mr. MacHinery. It's been very interesting talking to you, but I'm a busy man. What can I do for you?'

'A job,' said Joe.

'A job?'

'That's right. A start, a wee number; you know the drill.'

'We're looking for mechanics. Have you any experience?'

'Do you mean the bi-carbs, cam-head over-shafts and that sort of stuff? Oh yes.'

'In that case you can fix the Renault. The clutch is broken.'

'A Renault. What colour are they again? Don't tell me. A Renault — that's one of these American jobs.'

The manager was gone. Joe studied the name on each vehicle, then opened a passenger door. A clutch was obviously something you held. He turned on the headlights, flicked switches and pressed buttons for the windscreen wipers and washers. As far as he could see only the steering wheel was working and it was a bit stiff. There was a metal arm sticking up from the floor and it didn't look in the right position. It should be flat, thought Joe, and there was a place for your hand. Joe pushed, but the gear lever would not lie flat. He fetched a hammer, held the knob on the lever steady then hit his thumb squarely on the nail.

His screams filled the garage. No one asked what happened, for he was out cold. He wakened in hospital with his thumb bandaged and his arm in a sling. 'It's dangerous work being a motor mechanic,' he told the nurses. 'And you should see the smell.'

A week later Joe was back at work. He wore the bandage as a medal for half an hour's service. If anything, there were even more cars than before.

'Pleased to see you back,' said the manager. 'Look at the work we've got. The clutch on that Viva's broken. Do you think you could fix it.'

'The Viva,' said Joe. 'To be honest, I'm not used to working on these Italian motors.'

The manager was gone. He's a very impatient man, thought Joe.

Half an hour later he found a Viva, then spent two hours looking for the clutch. He looked under the car, inside the bonnet and even raked out the boot; but no one would want to hold anything in these places. The obvious place was inside the car.

42

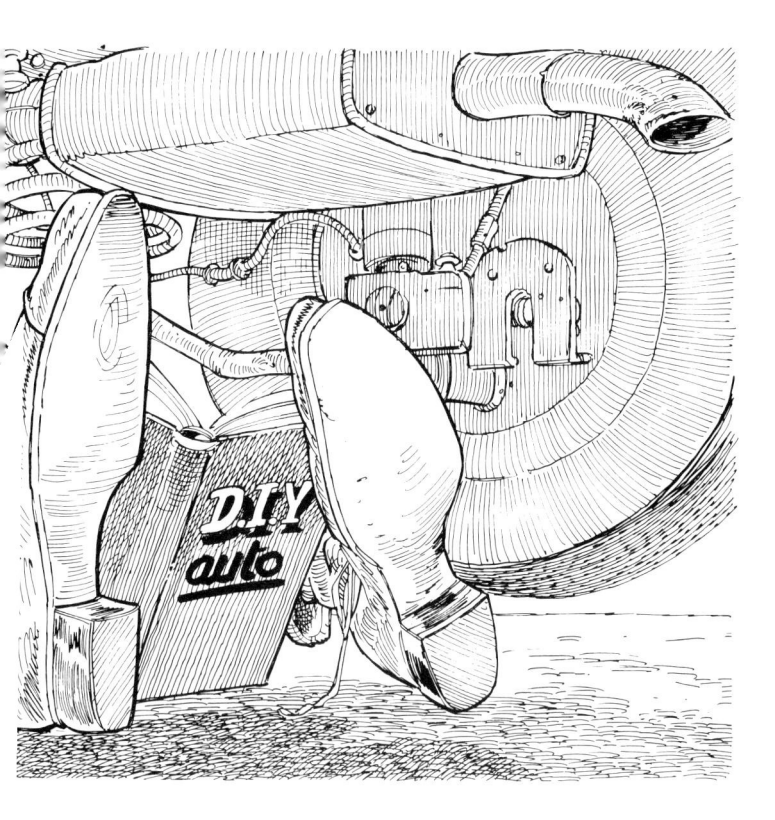

He checked that the indicators worked, the cigar lighter nearly burned his nose and the horn chased a cat who was sleeping on the roof. It had to be that metal thing sticking up, so he pushed the handbrake flat then noticed the car rolling back over his foot.

The hospital bed was warm, the food regular and the nurses listened to Joe's battle with machinery. He enjoyed his week's stay, thanked the staff and sold some blades before he left. Joe spent the next three weeks thinking about his accidents and discussing work with whoever would listen. 'This job's killing me,' he told them.

Eventually he returned to the garage, mended, enthusiastic but a wee bit cautious. He hoped they would take him off the heavy jobs. A bit of light work would sort him out.

The boss welcomed him back warmly. 'That Rover's just come in for repair. I think the cylinders are knocking a bit and the clutch is a bit stiff. I wonder if . . .'

'Oh here! A minute, pal,' shouted Joe. 'Am I the only guy around here who can fix clutches!'

> It was so cold here last winter my red mini turned blue.

The Kluge Maker

When Murgatroyd enlisted in the US Navy he made practically perfect scores on all the tests they gave him. The officer who interviewed him was very impressed and asked what his occupation had been.

'Kluge maker,' Murgatroyd replied.

The officer did not want to admit to such an extremely intelligent young man that he did not know what a kluge maker was. So he wrote down 'kluge maker' on Murgatroyd's record.

Murgatroyd went through training camp with flying colours. When he was interviewed about his next assignment, he also told that officer that he had been a kluge maker. And that officer also did not want to admit that he had never heard of one.

'I'll make you a Kluge Maker First Class,' he said. Of course, there is no such rating in the Navy, but with such an intelligent young man this seemed an exceptional case.

Murgatroyd was sent to Boston where he reported as a Kluge Maker First Class on the USS *Nymph*, which was going out on one of its first trips. It was a rough trip, the weather was bad, and the crew really worked hard. But Murgatroyd just sat.

When they got back to Boston, the captain of the ship was pretty angry at him and accused him of not doing a thing the whole trip.

'Well,' said Murgatroyd, 'I'm a kluge maker. And I certainly couldn't make kluges without anything to make them with.'

'What do you need?' asked the captain.

Murgatroyd sat up all night and made a long list — screws, bolts, hammers, axes, wire, batteries, iron, steel — the longest list you ever saw. They had to send all over the place to get the stuff. In fact, with the weight of all the kluge-making equipment, the ship listed to starboard when it went out again.

But Murgatroyd didn't do anything more on this trip than on the last one until the captain announced that the next morning an admiral would inspect the ship — and that the admiral was interested in kluges. The captain told Murgatroyd that he'd better have a kluge ready — or else.

When the admiral made his inspection the next morning he said to Murgatroyd, 'I understand you have been making kluges.'

'That's right, sir,' Murgatroyd replied.

'Well, let's see one.'

Murgatroyd opened his hand and there was the weirdest-looking thing you ever saw — with wires and springs sticking out in every direction.

Now the admiral had never seen a kluge before. But like the others he did not want to appear ignorant. He coughed warily and said, 'It looks like a perfect kluge. But if it's a perfect kluge, it should work perfectly. Let's see it work.'

Murgatroyd walked straight to the side of the ship and dropped the kluge overboard.

And when it hit the water it went — Kkluuge!

The High Divers

You ask me why I'm bunged up this way, going on crutches, both arms busted and what may still be a fractured skull. The doc ain't sure about that yet. I'll live, I guess, but I don't know what for. I can't never be a high diver no more. I'll go to selling razor blades, like as not, and there's plenty doing that already.

Eddie La Breen is to blame for it all. High diving was an easy and high-paying profession before he tried to root me and every other performer out of it. I would go travelling in the summer with a carnival and my high dive would be a free feature attraction. The local merchants would kick in for signs to put on my ladder and advertise their goods. Sometimes I'd make a little spiel from the top of the ladder just before I dived off into the tank.

Eddie La Breen called himself the 'Human Seal.' He bragged that he could dive higher into shallower water than any man alive. I was pretty good myself, being billed as Billie the Dolphin, Spectacular and Death-defying High Diver Extraordinary.

I'm doing all right with Miller's Great Exposition Shows, using a twenty-five foot ladder and diving into a ten-foot tank. Big crowds of people would come from miles around to see me and not a soul ever seemed dissatisfied until we happened to be playing Omaha on a lot over ten blocks away from where Eddie La Breen is playing with Baker's World's Fair Shows.

Just when I come up out of the tank and start to take a bow one night, I hear somebody say: 'That ain't nothing. You ought to see Eddie La Breen over on Farnum Street diving twice as high into water half as deep.'

I found out it's so. Eddie has been diving into five feet of water from a fifty-foot ladder, and Mr. Miller threatens to let me go if I can't do as well.

It sure looked high when I got up there and I could feel my nose scraping on the bottom of the tank just as I made the upturn. But I'm no slouch at the high dive myself, and Eddie La Breen ain't going to outdo me if I can help it.

I added the fire act to my dive, too, and most of the time I could hardly see where to dive. For the fire act you have a little bit of gasoline pouring into the tank. It stays right on top of the water and when you fire it, it makes a fearful sight, splashing fire in every direction when you hit the water.

Eddie sends me word that I might as well give up. 'I'm going to dive next from a thousand feet into a tank of solid concrete,' he says, 'and I'll do it while playing the ukulele, eating raw liver, and keeping perfect time. Why, when I was a kid of ten, I could dive off a silo into dew in the grass, bellybuster, and never even grunt when I lit.'

He didn't quite do what he said, but he did enough. He raised his ladder to a hundred feet, and kept only two and a half feet of water in the tank.

I practised and practised and got a few bruises, but I cut that depth to two feet and raised my ladder to a hundred and fifty feet.

By this time Eddie sent word he was good and mad, and he's going to call himself the Minnow. 'You know how a minnow just skitters along on top of a pond,' he says. 'Well, that's the way. I'll light on that tank. From two hundred feet I'll dive into six inches of water and just skim off without hardly making a bubble.'

If ever a man practised hard to make a shallow dive, that was me. I did that minnow dive in four inches of water from a height of two hundred fifty feet, lit right on my feet after barely touching the water, and didn't even muss my hair.

When Eddie makes it from three hundred feet into three inches, I'm a little put out, but I don't give up. I tell Miller to get me a good heavy bath mat and soak it

47

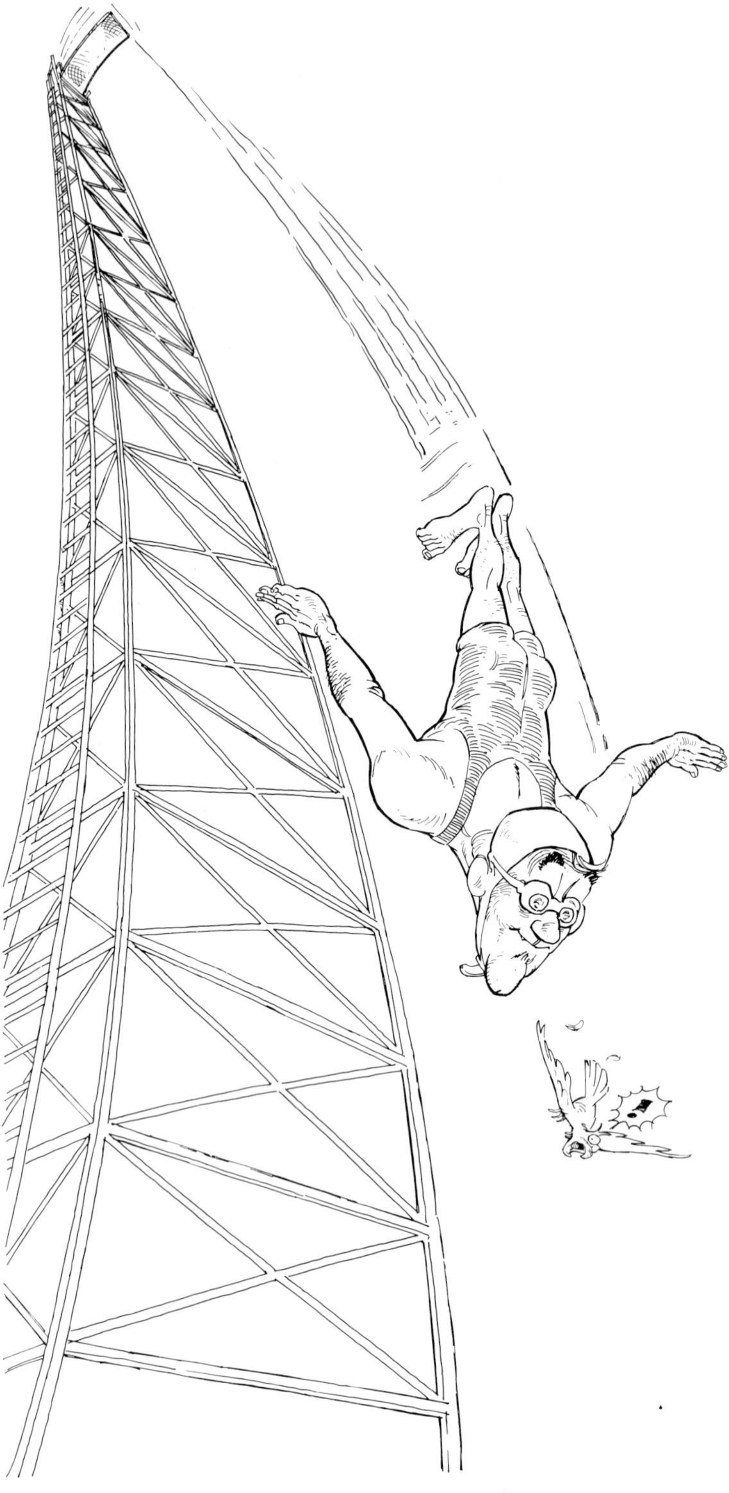

good all day. First time I hit that mat it sort of knocked me dizzy. You know how it is when you have the breath knocked out of you and all you can do is croak like a frog. But I got better and better at it until I hardly puffed at all.

I beat Eddie La Breen fair and square but he wasn't man enough to take it or admit it like a man. He showed that he was rotten to the core and treacherous from the word go.

We were playing Sheboygan, Wisconsin, and I had no idea that Eddie was anywhere within miles. I had heard that Barker had told him to pack up and get out when I bested him.

When I hit that bath mat that night, I thought my time had come. That was six months ago, and look at me now. Still on crutches and lucky if I ever get off of them.

Well, sir, I don't know anybody but Eddie who wanted to do me dirt. They had soaked my heavy bath mat in water all day the same as usual, but they must have let it get out of their sight sometime or other, because somebody had wrung it out practically dry.

That's the way I had it. I heard somebody say later that a man answering the description of Eddie La Breen had been seen lurking around the show grounds that evening. And if he didn't do it, who did?

The Fish Merchant

When he was a small boy, Bert Williams lived on the bank of a creek running at the foot of a mountain whose summit was, he said, 'seven thousand feet high.' Every morning, he would catch a string of fish in the brook and start up the mountainside where the white people lived.

'One mornin', bright 'n early, I starts up the mountain with my string of fish an' I comes to the fus' house, but they didn't want no fish. So I go on up higher to the secon' house, but they don't want no fresh fish nuther, an' I keep on climbin' higher 'n higher up that mountain, but none of the white folks wants fresh fish that mornin'. I continues till I reach the top, seven thousan' feet high, an' there I see a ole white man standin' at the do' of his little house.

'I walks over to him an' I say, "Mister, you want some fresh fish?" He says to me, he says, "No, I don't want no fish today."

'Well, there's nothin' left for me to do but climb down that seven thousan' feet mountain, an' when I'm most down to the bottom I hear a rumblin', an' when I look up I see a big lan'slide comin' down, an' pretty soon it hits me, an' down I go with tons of rocks 'n stones 'n dirt 'n tree-branches 'n whatall. At the foot of the mountain, by the creek, I digs myse'f out an' looks up to see if the whole mountain done come down with me, but what do I see but that ole white man, standin' on the plum top, an' beckonin' to me to come on back. So I says to myse'f, "Praise the Lawd, that white man done went an' changed his mind."

'So I clum' back up that seven thousan' feet mountain, all the way to the top an' I walks over to him with my string of fish.

'He don't say nothin' for a minute, an' then he says to me. . . .

"An' I won't be needin' any fish tomorrer neither!" '

Lazy! Why we've got a cockerel that's so lazy he waits for the one on the next farm to crow then nods his head.

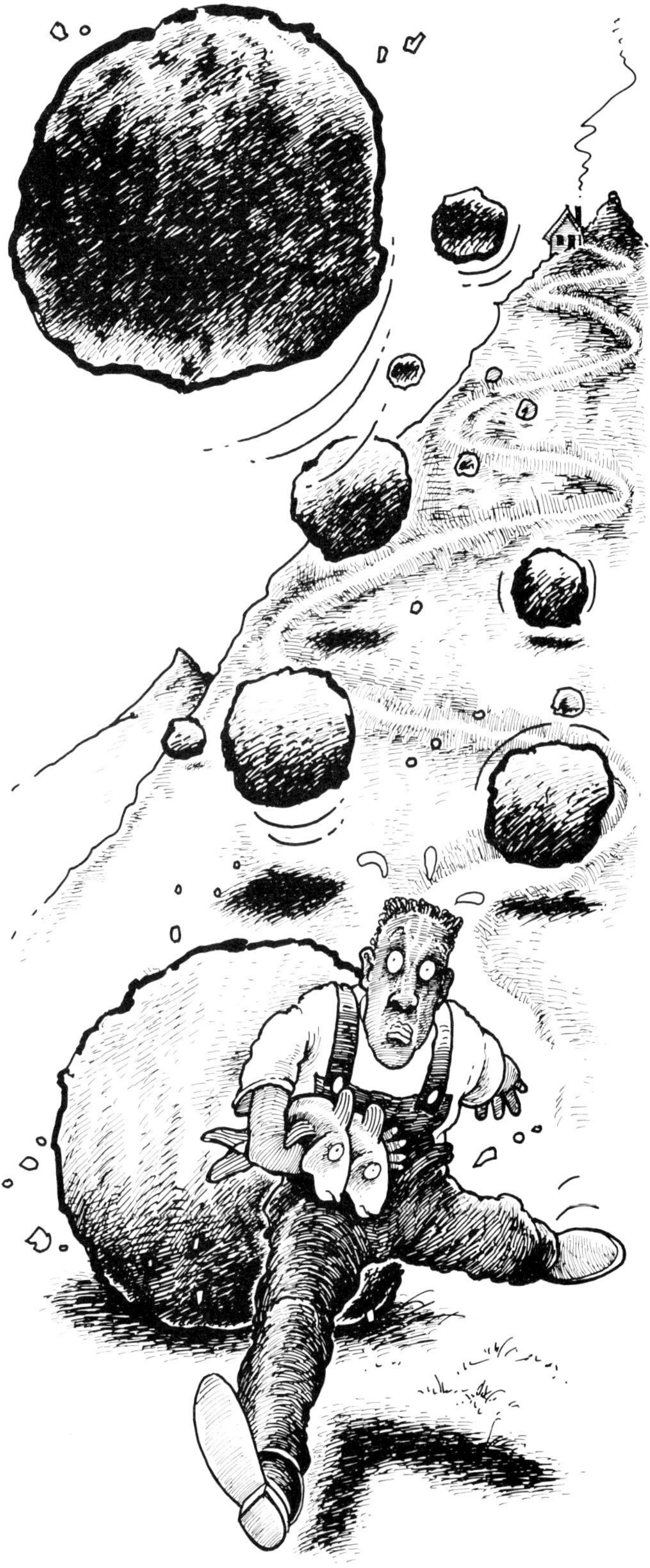

The Yankee Painter

A person who kept an inn by the roadside went to a painter, who for a time had set up his easel not a hundred miles from Ontario, and inquired for what sum the painter would paint him a bear for a signboard. It was to be a real good one, that would attract customers.

'Fifteen dollars!' replied the painter.

'That's too much!' said the inn-keeper; 'Tom Larkins will do it for ten.'

The painter cogitated for a moment. He did not like that this rival should get a commission in preference to himself, although it was only for a signboard.

'Is is to be a wild or tame bear?' he enquired.

'A wild one to be sure.'

'With a chain or without one?' again asked the painter.

'Without a chain!'

'Well, I will paint you a wild bear, without a chain, for ten dollars!'

The bargain was struck, the painter set to work, and in due time sent home the signboard, on which he had painted a huge and very ferocious brown bear. The signboard was the admiration of all the neighbourhood, and drew plenty of customers to the inn; and the inn-keeper knew not whether to congratulate himself more upon the possession of so attractive a sign, or on having secured it for the small sum of ten dollars. Time slipped on, his barrels were emptied and his pockets filled. Everything went on thrivingly for three weeks, when one night there arose one of those violent storms of rain and wind, thunder and lightning, which are so common in North America, and which pass over with almost as much rapidity as they rise. When the inn-keeper awoke next morning, the sun was shining, the birds singing, and all the traces of the storm had passed away. He looked up anxiously to ascertain that his sign was safe. There it was sure enough, swinging to and fro as usual, but the bear had disappeared. The inn-keeper could hardly believe his eyes; full of anger and surprise, he ran to the painter, and related what had happened.

The painter looked up coolly from his work.
'Was it a wild bear or a tame one?'
'A wild bear.'
'Was it chained or not?'
'I guess not.'
'Then,' cried the painter, triumphantly, 'how could you expect a wild bear to remain in such a storm as that of last night without a chain?'

The inn-keeper had nothing to say against so conclusive an argument, and finally agreed to give the painter fifteen dollars to paint him a wild bear with a chain, that would not take to the woods in the next storm.

To prevent the bear from running off, this time the painter used oil paint instead of water colours.

V

Lizzie's Lion 54
Léon and the Lion 57
The Pet Rattlesnake 59
The Mare's Egg 60
The Horse 61
Grant's Tame Trout 62
Blue Cloud's Cat 64
Pablo Romero Roped a Bear 65

Lizzy's lion

Lizzy had a lion
    With a big, bad roar,
And she kept him in the bedroom
    By the closet-cupboard door;

Lizzy's lion wasn't friendly,
    Lizzy's lion wasn't tame —
Not unless you learned to call him
    By his Secret Lion Name.

One dark night, a rotten robber
    With a rotten robber mask
Snuck in through the bedroom window —
    And he didn't even ask.

And he brought a bag of candy
    That was sticky-icky-sweet,
Just to make friends with a lion
    (If a lion he should meet).

First he sprinkled candy forwards,
    Then he sprinkled candy back;
Then he picked up Lizzy's piggy-bank
    And stuck it in his sack.

But as the rotten robber
   Was preparing to depart,
Good old Lizzy's lion wakened
   With a snuffle and a start.

And he muttered, 'Candy? — piffle!'
   And he rumbled, 'Candy? — pooh!'
And he gave the rotten robber
   An experimental chew.

Then the robber shooed the lion,
   Using every name he knew;
But each time he shooed, the lion
   Merely took another chew.

It was: 'Down, Fido! Leave, Leo!
   Shoo, you good old boy!'
But the lion went on munching
   With a look of simple joy.

It was: 'Stop, Mopsy! Scram, Sambo!
  This is a disgrace!'
But the lion went on lunching
  With a smile upon his face.

Then old Lizzy heard the rumble,
  And old Lizzy heard the fight,
And old Lizzy got her slippers
  And turned on the bedroom light.

There was robber on the toy-shelf!
  There was robber on the rug!
There was robber in the lion
  (Who was looking rather smug)!

But old Lizzy wasn't angry,
  And old Lizzy wasn't rough.
She simply said the Secret Name:
  '*Lion!* — that's enough.'

Then old Lizzy and her Lion
  Took the toes & tum & head,
And they put them in the garbage,
  And they both went back to bed.

León and the Lion

There is a little village sitting on the edge of a jungle somewhere in the world, where the people live very happily most of the time. But one day not long ago, a big lion came walking into the village and ate a man.

He went away then, but a few days later he came back and ate two men. About a week later he came walking into the village and ate three men.

So three of the bravest hunters went into the jungle to hunt the lion. But they never came back. Nobody ever found out what happened.

More hunters went into the jungle to hunt the lion — and they never came back.

This happened several times, and at last the people of the village were afraid to go hunting for the lion. And the lion kept coming into the village and eating the people.

At last the king sent a messenger through all the world for somebody to please come and kill the lion.

First came some Englishmen. They wore short pants and sun helmets; and the first thing they did was sit down and make tea. While they were drinking the tea, the lion came and ate them.

Next came some Germans. They knew all about lions from studying in books, and they had made a map showing just how they were going to hunt this lion and catch it.

But while they were studying the map, the lion came and ate them.

Next came some Frenchmen. They were very polite. One of them saw the lion and pointed his gun at it, then suddenly remembered his manners.

'After you!' he said, and bowed to his companion.

'Oh, no! After you!' said the other fellow. And while they were bowing to each other, the lion came and ate them.

Next came some Americans. They had wonderful big guns. But while they were polishing and oiling the guns, the lion came and ate them, too.

Then a young Mexican boy came along. He was very young and very handsome. His name was León.

The first thing he did was lean a big convex mirror up against a tree at the edge of the forest. The lion came along and saw himself in it. He thought, Oh, what a big fierce lion I am! So he went into the village and ate four people.

The king was very angry. He thought that León had just made matters worse.

'Just wait, your majesty. Just wait,' León begged.

The next day León leaned another mirror against the tree. This one was not quite so big, not quite so convex as the first one. The lion didn't look quite so big to himself. That day he ate only two people.

The next day León put a flat mirror against the tree. When the lion looked at himself, he thought he looked like just any old lion, so that day he ate only one silly old woman.

The next day León put up a smaller mirror — a little bit concave.

When the lion came along and looked, he saw a fairly small lion in there. That day he just stood on the edge of the village and didn't feel very hungry.

The next day León's mirror was smaller yet, and more concave. When the lion saw himself in it, he felt so insignificant that he just slunk back into the jungle.

The next day León leaned a very small mirror against the tree — a tiny mirror, very concave.

When the lion looked into it he saw such a *little* lion that he thought he was a kitten! Then León came along and put him in a paper bag and took him to the king.

The king and the people of the village were so happy that they had a big feast that night, and León went home to Mexico with lots of money.

The Pet Rattlesnake

When I was just a wee lad I wanted to be a cowboy and it was then that I found out what a swell friend a rattlesnake could be. I was riding through a pass one day when I saw a rattler pinned under a stone: dismounting, I made ready to kill him, but changed my mind. Didn't seem fair. So I pushed the rock off and went home. As I went along I kept hearing funny noises behind me and looked back and saw it was that silly snake. It came right to my cabin and I opened some canned milk; and that snake drank it all, and you could just see the gratitude in his eyes. He stayed around and got so friendly he slept under my bed.

One night I was sleeping soundly when a bang awakened me. I could hear someone panting and struggling, so I grabbed my gun and said, 'Hands up! If you move it wouldn't surprise me if I shot something!' A loud voice yelled, 'For God's sake, take this damned thing off of me!' I lit a candle. There, sprawled on the floor, was a guy who had sneaked in to steal my gold dust. But my rattler had wrapped himself around the man's leg and the leg of the table — and had his tail through the keyhole, rattling for the sheriff!

The Mare's Egg

Dunnamany year ago, two chaps what had come from Lunnon — a pleäce where all de men be as wise as owls — met a h'old Sussex man what was doddling along a roäd near his village wid a pumpkin under his arm. An' dese two Lunnon chaps didn't know what dis pumpkin was, as dey had never sin de loikes of un afore. So one on 'em says to de other, he says, 'Let's see what dis here ol' fellow's got under 'is arm.'

So dey goos up to un an' says, 'Good marnin', mister,' dey says.

'Good marnin',' says de ol' chap, friendly-like.

'What be dat under yer arm?' says de Lunnoners.

'Dat be a mare's egg,' says de ol' man.

'Dat so?' says de Lunnoners, believin' un loike lambs, 'We've never sin one so foine afore.'

'Yes,' says de ol' chap, 'dere be a mort o' common ones aroun', but dis 'ere one be a thoroughbred, an' dat's why 'tis so gurt an' foine.'

'Will you sell un?' says de Lunnoners.

'Wall,' says de ol' chap, hesitating-like, 'I doän't mind if I do, only I be dubbersome if you'll gi' me what I wants fur un; I ain't a mind to take less dan a golden sovrin' fur dis 'ere thoroughbred mare's egg.'

So arter dunnamuch talk dese 'ere Lunnon chaps dey gi' un what he axed, an' so he guv 'em de pumpkin, an' he says, 'Mind ye carry it careful,' he says, ''cos 'twill hatch pretty soon, I rackon.'

'All right,' says de Lunnoners, 'we'll be careful.'

So off dey goos over de fields wud de mare's egg; and prensley him what was a-carryin' of it ketches his foot in a hole in de groun' so dat he dropped de pumpkin all of a sudden, an' dat starts a hare from de bushes, so dat it rip-an'-run down de hill. De chaps was dat vlothered dat dey was sure dat de mare's egg was hatched, so dey shouts out to some men what was workin' at de bottom of de hill, 'Hi! Stop our colt! Stop our colt!'

We fed frozen flames to the hens and had hard-boiled eggs for three months.

The Horse

'Is there anything wrong with it?' he asked.

'Just look at him, sir. As fine a piece of horseflesh as you'll see in many a year. Gentle, good disposition, moves like a dream and as strong as a horse. Jumps well. Doesn't pull.'

'So what *is* wrong with him? If he's as good as you say, you'd be wanting more for him than the price you've just quoted me.'

'Melons, sir, melons.'

'Melons! What on earth do you mean?'

'Every time he sees a melon he sits on it. Can't explain it, sir, just a habit he's got. Nothing to do with his breeding. He's a marvellous horse as you can see, and his papers are all in order, but as for melons — you just have to keep them out of his sight.'

And as the man really didn't expect to come across many melons up in the hills, and as the price really was exceptionally good, he paid the dealer, mounted the horse, and set out for home.

They were crossing a stream when the horse sat down.

'That's not funny!' shouted the man, now soaking wet, as he tried to pull the horse up. 'I don't believe there are melons in the middle of the stream. What are you doing? Playing jokes, or something?' And he tried again to heave the horse out, but he couldn't. Pulling, pushing, coaxing, and even kicking all had the same effects: the horse sat unmoved in the middle of the stream.

Finally, the man squelched back to the market and found the dealer.

'Now look here,' he said. 'That horse you sold me. For one thing he seems to think melons grow in rivers and for another I can't move him.'

'Oh my goodness!' said the dealer, 'I'm very sorry, sir, but I forgot to tell you. He sits on fish, too.'

There's one stream I know that winds about so much you can't jump across it. No matter how often you try you always land on the side you started from.

Grant's Tame Trout

'Well, it was this way. Nine year ago the eleventh day of last June, I was out fishin' when I ketched a trout 'bout six inches long. I never see a more intelligent lookin' little feller — high forehead, smooth face, round, dimpled chin, and a most uncommon bright, sparkling, knowin' eye.

'I always allowed that with patience and cunning a real young trout (when they gets to a weight of 10 or 15 pounds there ain't no teachin' them nothin') could be tamed jest like a dog or cat.

'There was a little water in the boat and he swims around in it all right till I goes ashore and then I gets a tub we had, made of the half of a pork barrel, fills it with water and bores a little small hole through the side close down to the bottom and stops the hole with a peg.

'I sets this tub away back in a dark corner of the camp and every night after the little fellow gets asleep I slip in, in my stockin' feet and pulls out the peg softly and lets out jest a little mite of the water. I does this night after night so mighty sly that the little chap never suspected nothin' and he was a-livin' hale and hearty for three weeks on the bottom of that tub as dry as a cook stove, and then I knowed he was fit for trainin'.

'So I took him out o' doors and let him wiggle awhile on the path and soon got to feedin' him out of my hand. Pretty soon after that, when I walked somewhat slow he could follow me right good all round the clearin', but sometimes his fins did get ketched up in the brush jest a mite and I had to go back and swamp out a little trail for him; bein' a trout, of course he could easy follow a spotted line.

'Well, as time went on, he got to follerin' me most everywhere and hardly ever lost sight of me, and me and him was great friends, sure enough.

'Near about sundown one evening, I went out to the spring back of the camp to get some butter out of a pail, and, of course, he comes trottin' along behind. There was no wind that night, I remember, and I could hear his poor little fins a-raspin' on the chips where we'd been gettin' out logs in the cedar swamp. Well, sir, he follered me close up and came out onto the logs across the brook and jest as I was a-stoopin' down over the pail I heard a kee-plunk! behind me and Gorry! if he hadn't slipped through a chink between them logs and was drownded before my very eyes before I could reach him, so he was.

'Of course I was terribly cut up at first — I couldn't do a stroke of work for three weeks — but I got to thinkin' that as it was comin' on cold (it was in late November then) and snow would soon be here and he, poor little cuss, wasn't rugged enough for snow-shoein' and he couldn't foller me afoot all winter no how, and as he couldn't live without me, mebby it was jest as well after all he was took off that way. Do you know, Mister, some folks around here don't believe a word of this, but if you'll come down to the spring with me, right now, I'll show you the very identical chink he dropped through that night, so I will. I've never allowed anyone to move it. No, sir! nor I never will.'

Blue Cloud's Cat

Blue Cloud of the Au Sable Ottawa Indians had a hunting cat. There were many hunting dogs in the community, but Blue Cloud had the only hunting cat. The cat got so good that Blue Cloud never had to hunt for his meat. One morning he would have a rabbit at the doorstep, the next morning he would have a partridge.

Then one morning the cat didn't show up. For several mornings he didn't appear, and Blue Cloud had to start hunting again. In about two weeks the cat came back with all his ribs showing and a front leg gone. He had been caught in a trap and had taken two weeks to break out, leaving that leg in the process.

Blue Cloud fed the cat generously, and he regained his strength. He still limped of course, so the Ottawa thought he would remedy the cripple; he whittled out a peg leg for him. With that peg leg the cat got around almost as good as ever. Soon he was bringing rabbits to the door again.

'I wonder how that cat manages to catch a rabbit,' Blue Cloud said to his wife.

'Why don't you trail him and find out?' she suggested.

So one morning Blue Cloud set out to watch his hunter cat. The cat wandered off around a hill and began circling a hollow stump. 'There's a rabbit in that stump,' thought Blue Cloud.

Sure enough, pretty soon a rabbit dashed out of the stump. The cat pounced on it and beat it to death with his peg leg.

There are so many rabbits on the farm you have to pull them out of their burrows to get the ferrets in.

Pablo Romero Roped a Bear

A long time ago a certain bear that had been offended by a vaquero caught him and while chewing on him found his blood so good tasting that he ate the vaquero up. After that he lay in wait for men. Frequently he was shot at, but no bullet ever seemed to harm him.

Because of a white spot on his black-haired front, this bear was called Star Breast. He haunted glades and woods around a fine spring of water where two mountain trails crossed. The place was called La Quiparita. All travel over this part of the country was by horses and mules and all travellers favoured the fine camping grounds at La Quiparita — wood, water, grass, and shelter by the big trees near at hand. In time the place came to be avoided because of the number of people Star Breast had destroyed there.

Now, a vaquero who worked on a ranch a long way off and had often heard of Star Breast was very brave and very ambitious. One day while he had another vaquero were hunting strayed horses in the Quiparita country, they saw the tracks of Star Breast — tracks so enormous that no man of the camps could mistake them for the tracks of any other bear.

'Listen,' said Pablo Romero, 'I am going to kill Star Breast. I know that it is useless to try to shoot him and we have no guns anyhow. But I shall rope him and choke him to death the way we rope Indians and choke them. I am riding as good a roping horse as a reata was ever thrown from. He has the strength of ten bulls in him. This rawhide reata is new. It would hold an elephant.'

Pablo Romero's companion pleaded with him not to think of such a foolhardy undertaking. 'Why, don't you know,' he said, 'that if Star Breast is proof against bullets he will be proof against rawhide. Right now he hides in those bushes listening to us and preparing to come after us. Instead of riding farther toward him, let us go the other way.'

'No,' replied Pablo Romero, 'in this country lead is not superior to rawhide. A good roper, a good roping horse, and a good rope can conquer anything that breathes.'

Pablo Romero would not be turned. His companion finally consented to stay and watch the roping from a distance. They rode on toward the bushes and, sure enough, as they approached, Star Breast emerged. He stood on his hind legs, waving his great hairy arms, rumbled a great roar, and then came on. The horses ridden by the vaqueros tried to stampede, but Pablo Romero, by untying his reata from the horn of the saddle and playing out a loop, persuaded his horse to keep going. A good roping horse can hardly be stopped when he realizes that the rope is being prepared for action. The other vaquero had halted.

He saw Pablo Romero fasten one end of the reata to his saddle. He saw him with swinging loop dash toward Star Breast, who had halted and was again reared on his hind legs. Then he saw the loop fall over Star Breast's head, while man and rider dashed on. When the end of the rope was reached, the horse was jerked back and the bear was jerked down. The loop had caught him under one arm and around the neck. Almost instantly the horse whirled so that he could get a better pull, and at the same time the bear recovered his upright position.

And now came a desperate manoeuvre between a gigantic, fierce, powerful and cunning bear at one end of the rope and an expert horse ridden by an expert rider at the other end. Several times the bear was jerked down. Had the loop not been under his arm, the pull about his neck would no doubt have choked him. The bear soon learned that by grasping the rope with his hands he could break the force of the jerks. Once he caught the tough rawhide in his teeth just at the instant it was tightening. A tooth was jerked out and he howled with rage. He did not catch the reata with his teeth again. He began to go forward up the rope toward the horse. As the length of the rope between the animals grew shorter, the horse had a shorter distance in which to run and therefore could not jerk so hard. He could not jerk the rope out of the bear's hand. He was panting hard.

Pablo Romero was a brave vaquero. He would not quit his horse. He had no gun of any kind to shoot. The rope was knotted so tightly about his saddle horn that he could not loosen it. Worse, on this day he had no knife with which to cut it. Had his companion been very brave, perhaps he might have roped the bear also and have pulled him away from his friend.

He was not that brave. Besides, as he said, this roping contest was not his.

At last, panting and frothing, Star Breast got up to horse and man. Now the vaquero who was watching saw a strange thing. He saw Star Breast reach up and drag Pablo Romero from the saddle. He saw him take the rope off his neck, coil it up, and tie it to the saddle horn. Then he saw him mount the horse and, with the limp form of Pablo Romero across the saddle in front of him, ride off into the brush! That was the last ever seen of Pablo Romero or of Pablo Romero's horse.

VI

If You Want to Live for Ever   68
The Cake   70
To Save Time   71
The Lobster   72
The Patcham Treacle Mines   74

If You Want to Live for ever

There is the story of the Kasrilevkite who got tired of starving in Kasrilevka and went out into the wide world to seek his fortune. He left the country, wandered far and wide, and finally reached Paris. There, naturally, he wanted to see Rothschild. For how can a Jew come to Paris and not visit Rothschild? But they didn't let him in. 'What's the trouble?' he wants to know. 'Your coat is torn,' they tell him.

'You fool,' says the Jew. 'If I had a good coat, would I have gone to Paris?'

It looked hopeless. But a Kasrilevkite never gives up. He thought a while and said to the doorman: 'Tell your master that it isn't an ordinary beggar who has come to his door, but a Jewish merchant, who has brought him a piece of goods such as you can't find in Paris for any amount of money.'

Hearing this, Rothschild became curious and asked that the merchant be brought to him.

'*Sholom aleichem,*' said Rothschild.
'*Aleichem sholom,*' said the merchant.
'Take a seat. And where do you come from?'
'I come from Kasrilevka.'
'What good news do you bring?'
'Well, Mr Rothschild, they say in our town that you are not so badly off. If I had only half of what you own, or only a third, you would still have enough left. And

honours, I imagine, you don't lack either, for people always look up to a man of riches. Then what do you lack? One thing only — eternal life. That is what I have to sell you.'

When Rothschild heard this he said, 'Well, let's get down to business. What will it cost me?'

'It will cost you —' here the man stopped to consider — 'it will cost you — three hundred roubles.'

'Is that your best price?'

'My very best. I could have said a lot more than three hundred. But I said it, so it's final.'

Rothschild said no more, but counted out three hundred roubles, one by one.

Our Kasrilevkite slipped the money into his pocket, and said to Rothschild: 'If you want to live for ever, my advice to you is to leave this noisy, busy Paris, and move to our town of Kasrilevka. There you can never die, because since Kasrilevka has been a town, no rich man has ever died there.'

> The land is so poor we have to put baking powder in the coffins so that people can rise again on Judgement Day.

The Cake

A man went to a baker and asked him to bake a cake in the form of the letter S. The baker said he would need a week to prepare the necessary tins. The customer agreed, and returned a week later. Proudly the baker showed him the cake.

'Oh, but you misunderstood me,' the customer said. 'You have made it a block letter and I wanted script.'

'Well,' said the baker, 'if you can wait another week I can bake one in script.'

When the customer returned, he sorrowfully informed the baker that he had wanted the letter in pink icing and not in green.

'Sorry,' said the baker, 'but you'll have to give me another week to change it.'

A week later the customer came back, and was delighted with the cake.

'Exactly what I wanted.'

'Will you take it with you,' asked the baker, 'or shall I send it to your house?'

'Don't bother,' said the customer. 'I'll eat it right here.'

To Save Time

On the express train to Lublin, a young man stopped at the seat of an obviously prosperous merchant.

'Can you tell me the time?' he said.

The merchant looked at him and replied: 'Go to hell!'

'What? Why, what's the matter with you! I ask you a civil question, in a properly civil way, and you give me such an outrageous, rude answer! What's the idea?'

The merchant looked at him, sighed wearily, and said, 'Very well. Sit down and I'll tell you. You ask me a question. I have to give you an answer, no? You start a conversation with me — about the weather, politics, business. One thing leads to another. It turns out you're a Jew — I'm a Jew. I live in Lublin — you're a stranger. Out of hospitality, I ask you to my home for dinner. You meet my daughter. She's a beautiful girl — you're a handsome young man. So you go out together a few times — and you fall in love. Finally you come to ask for my daughter's hand in marriage. So why go to all that trouble. Let me tell you right now, young man, I won't let my daughter marry anyone who doesn't even own a watch!'

The Lobster

They were regulars. Same time, same table in the corner, same order: double scotch for the man and a half of bitter for each of the dogs. They stayed for twenty minutes, drinking slowly and with obvious enjoyment, then left quietly. Regular as clockwork, every evening weekends included. It wasn't long before the barman had their drinks ready when they came.

One evening the two dogs arrived on their own and went and sat in their usual corner. The barman gave them their usual drinks, which they consumed in their usual manner. Twenty minutes later they quietly left.

The same thing happened the next few nights, but at the end of the week the man again appeared with his dogs.

'I'm very grateful to you,' he said to the barman. 'They look forward to their evening drink and I didn't want to disappoint them just because I was ill.'

'That's quite all right, sir, I knew you would be back. And I only wish some of my other customers were as well-behaved as your dogs. A credit to you, they are.'

'Here's what I owe for the drinks, but to show how much I appreciate the way you looked after my dogs I've brought you something rather special. I hope you will accept it.'

And he placed a small lobster on the bar.

'Oh, thank you very much indeed, sir. I'll take it home for supper.'

'There's no need to do that. He's had his supper. Just put him to bed when you get back.'

In West Virginia the hills are so steep and the valleys so narrow dogs wag their tails up and down instead of sideways.

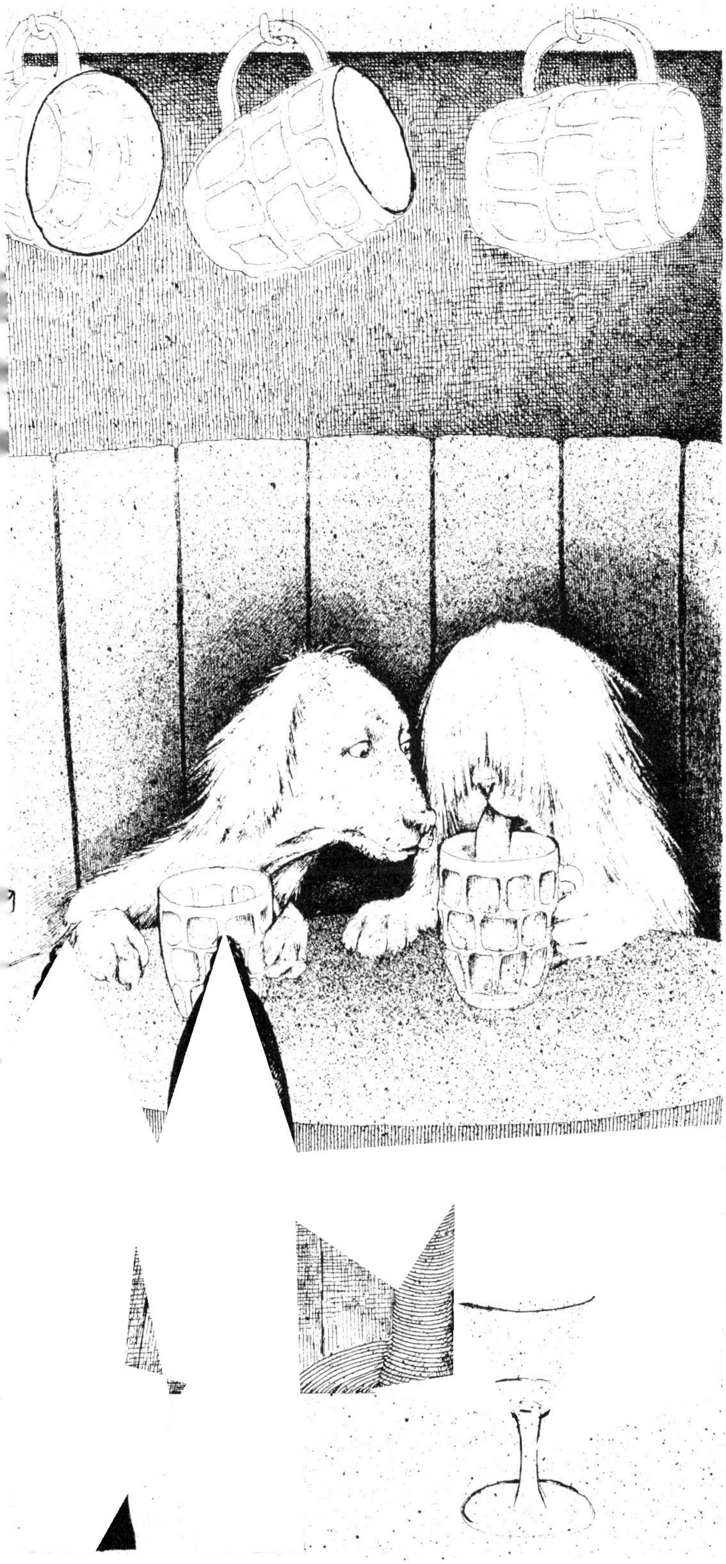

The Patcham Treacle Mines

The Treacle Mines at Patcham are one of our old Sussex industries, a link in a chain which has spanned the centuries back to the days when prehistoric monsters roamed the land. Millions of years ago, when England was a tropical country, before the Ice Age, sugar cane grew here. Year after year it grew, ripened and rotted unharvested, the molasses draining away down into the folds of the hills, where it accumulated above an impermeable layer of clay. The centuries passed, the colder weather came, and sugar cane no longer grew on the Downs, but the underground layer of treacle lay patiently waiting until in 1871 Peter Jones, a scientist who had long suspected its existence, sank the first shaft. The ensuing treacle gusher spouted for three days, covering the countryside for several miles around with a fine rain of treacle, until it was brought at last under control. Since that day the treacle mines have provided employment for many Patcham families, the jealously guarded privilege of free treacle (tins not provided) being handed down from father to son in the families of the original twenty employees.

During the war the treacle mines rendered sterling service to the Allied cause, eking out the sugar ration, so much so that it was found necessary to take down the old signs "To the Treacle Mines" and substitute others, in order to mislead possible enemy saboteurs; unfortunately these have never been restored, and the identity of the buildings is today still a mystery to many.

The treacle supply is not exhausted, and the demand for it still exists, so much so that the old buildings have recently been replaced with newer up-to-date ones. Patcham Treacle Mines are more than a tradition, more than an institution, for many Patcham families they are a way of life. They also provide remarkably good treacle.

> They're really mean. They make their pancakes so thin they've only got one side.

VII

The Horse who Played Cricket   75
The Cow Mechanic   77
The Scholarly Mouse   78
The Smart Dog   83
John and the Blacksnake   86

The Horse who Played Cricket

There was once a visiting cricket team — a town team — that went out to play against a country team. And just at the last moment as they got on to the bus, they got a message from one of the team that he had broken his leg and couldn't come. They hadn't a spare man, and they hadn't time to look for one, so the only thing was to hope that there might be some spare players in the home team, and they could borrow one. When they got to the place, the captain of the visiting team explained how it was, and asked the captain of the home team if he could borrow any member of the club for the game. 'I'm awfully sorry,' said the home captain, 'we're such a small club that all our members are playing. I don't know what we can do. Oh! I know, go and ask that old horse over there if he'll stand in for you. He's drawn the mower and the roller for years, and there isn't anything he doesn't know about cricket. He's a good-natured old chap; go over and ask him nicely, and I'm sure he'll consent.'

So the captain of the visiting team walked over to the horse, and he said, 'Excuse me, sir, the captain thinks you might be willing to oblige us. One of the team's failed at the last moment, and the captain thought you might be willing to play for us. We don't like to go home without a game at all.'

'Well, I'm terribly out of practice,' said the horse, 'but I don't like to be disobliging. I'll tell you what; put me down to bat last, and then I can't do much harm.'

So that was arranged. The home team won the toss, and they put the visiting team in to bat first. They may have been a small club, but every man of them was a cricketer, as the visiting team soon discovered. They had a couple of demon bowlers who knocked the wickets down like ninepins, and soon there were nine wickets down, with about twice as many runs. It was the old horse's turn to go in, and soon the visiting team's spirits began to rise, for he knocked those bowlers all over the field. The score went to twenty, thirty, forty, fifty, and it looked as if the old horse would stay there till he'd made his century, only unfortunately the tenth man got caught out, and that was the end of the innings. After this, the home team went in, and they soon showed they were as good at batting as they were at bowling, and the visiting captain put on every bowler they had, and they were all treated with contempt. At last, he went over to the old horse, who was fielding long-stop.

'You've done so well for us in the batting, sir,' he said, 'I wonder if you would try what you can do with the bowling?'

The old horse looked at him, and he threw back his head, and laughed and laughed. 'Bowling!' he said, 'who ever heard of a horse bowling at cricket?'

The Cow Mechanic

Lewis had given up. When his car spluttered to a halt miles, it seemed, from anywhere, he couldn't figure out what was wrong. He had plenty of petrol but the engine refused to start up again.

He opened the bonnet and wiggled various bits of wire about to check whether they were tight or loose. It still wouldn't start.

He kicked the wheels and slammed the boot. No good.

Now he stood with the bonnet up again looking in despair at all the complicated machinery. Why did they need all this just to make a simple thing like a car go? If they put less in there would be fewer things to go wrong.

'Have you checked the carburettor?' asked a voice behind him.

'Ah,' said Lewis, turning with relief, 'help at last!'

Apart from a cow, chewing thoughtfully a few yards away, there was no one there. He looked round quickly, then eyed the cow with deep suspicion.

'Er, did . . . did you, er, say something?' he asked.

'Yes,' said the cow. 'I said I thought you had carburettor trouble. Do you mind if I take a look?' She moved forward to peer under the bonnet.

Lewis had thought he was miles from anywhere but within ten minutes he was in a farmhouse kitchen telling the farmer what had happened.

'A Jersey?' asked the farmer.

'A *cow*!' Lewis insisted. 'Big thing. Chews all the time.'

'With a crumped horn?'

'That's the one!'

'Well,' said the farmer, 'I wouldn't pay much attention to that one if I were you. She doesn't know as much about cars as she thinks she does.'

> **The cattle get so thin it takes at least four to cast a shadow.**

77

The Scholarly Mouse

A studious young mouse immersed himself in his books and then declared in the presence of an ancient:

'I have found the way to the millennium!'

The aged mouse wiped a rheumy eye before replying scornfully, 'Everyone knows the way — we've known it for centuries — but no one yet has found a way of belling the cat.'

'Crude and unscientific!' said the studious young mouse. 'Hypnotism is the lurk.'

'All my eye!' said the old mouse. 'Hypnotize me — or whatever the verb is —'

The young mouse made a few passes with his right paw and left the ancient chewing a bit of soap under the delusion it was prize Limburger. He set his shoulders, made his way along the inside of the skirting-board, emerged from the hole and marched forthrightly across the carpet to where the ginger cat was sleeping by the fire.

When the mouse was about ten feet short the cat awoke. He blinked at the sight of the mouse coming on boldly towards him and told himself:

'I must be still dreaming! Obviously that last mouse was too much for me.'

'So will this one be!' said the studious young mouse in a resolute voice.

The cat sat up with a jerk then.

'You'll pardon the question, I hope,' he said silkily, 'but have I perhaps bitten you behind the ears on the occasion of an earlier meeting?'

'No,' said the mouse in a stern voice, still coming on.

'Extr'ordinary!' said the ginger cat. He shrugged his shoulders. 'Who am I to argue with my supper?'

The mouse concentrated hard, gathered the corners of his lids together until his eyes glittered like those of a villain in a Victorian melodrama, and made a couple of passes with his right paw, saying, 'Cat, you're very sleepy. You're very sleepy. You're very sleepy.'

'Oh, but I'm not a bit sl—' the cat started to say and then yawned.

'You see in front of you a large fierce dog!' said the mouse.

'By Gad, I believe you're right!' said the cat to himself. 'Extr'ordinary! Fierce, too!' His fur flew up on the back of his neck and he shook with fear. He went up four feet in the air, fell over on his back with funk, streaked out the door, out of the house and kept on going.

The young mouse's triumph was complete and the other mice in the house proclaimed him the saviour of their race; quite soon his fame had spread to other households where mice sought his help.

'I must help them,' said the young mouse. 'The good life is the right of all members of our race.'

He gave tirelessly of his services and liberated first whole streets and then whole suburbs.

Meanwhile, the ginger cat was in a cats' home and explaining his neurosis to other refugees:

'I could have sworn it was a mouse and then, by Gad, it was a mastiff with teeth as big as butchers' knives.'

'My experience was the same except it was an Alsatian,' said a tabby.

'An Irish wolfhound made me a displaced person!' said a Persian. 'I had the finest home in the world.'

'A bull-terrier frightened me out of seven of my lives,' said a tortoiseshell.

'A greyhound flummoxed me out of eight and a half,' said a black cat, weakly.

An albino cat, who had been listening to the conversation, now contributed:

'One common factor is that all of us saw, or thought we saw, a mouse, in the first place. It appears to me that some form of mass hysteria is at work.'

'Who's hysterical, by Gad!' cried the ginger cat.

'I'm the same as the next cat!' shouted the tabby.

'It's you that's hysterical!' cried the Persian to the albino.

'You read too much!' shouted the tortoiseshell. 'All that silly psychology stuff!'

'As you wish, gentlemen and idiots,' said the albino. 'I was trying to help. However, I see I must do it alone. I'm going back to beard the mastiff, the Alsatian, the Irish wolfhound, the bull-terrier, the greyhound — to say nothing of my own timber-wolf which I saw at dusk. Good afternoon, fellow psychotics!'

Outside in the street, however, the albino cat did not feel so brave, particularly as the afternoon sun blinded him. He bumped into lamp-posts and garbage tins, fell into gutters, tripped over stones and once narrowly escaped being run down by an animal ambulance with a load of hysterical cats.

'Those dolts at the home are more blind than I am!' the albino cat told himself and pressed on, resolutely.

In the late afternoon he drew near his former home. He was drawing a couple of deep breaths before entering when he caught the whiff of a mouse. It was the studious young mouse returning from extending the mouse millennium to another household.

'Just a moment, mouse,' said the albino cat, groping forward.

'One I've missed,' said the young mouse, under his breath. Aloud, he said, 'You're very sleepy. You're very sleepy. You're very sleepy.'

'I am rather,' said the albino cat. 'I've come miles and I'm in a bad temper — all because of those ignorant fools back in the cat's home. No progress will ever be made while members of our race despise study and sneer at book learning.'

'You see in front of you a big fierce dog!' said the mouse.

'Not a thing,' said the albino cat. 'As I was saying, it is a few choice spirits that are responsible for all the progress which is made in the world —'

'A big fierce dog!' repeated the mouse. He waved his paws excitedly and repeated, 'A big fierce dog!' coming to within a few inches of the cat.

'Eureka!' cried the albino cat. 'I've got it! I'm damned, a mouse that practises hypnotism!' He put out a paw and trapped the mouse. 'I wish I could see you, my friend. You're a choice spirit like myself.'

'Can't see me!' gasped the mouse. 'Oh, I'm undone!'

'I'm afraid so,' said the albino cat. 'Can't see a thing till the sun gets down.' He went on tenderly, 'I could love you, my friend, if Nature hadn't ruled otherwise.' He started to laugh. 'To think of how you fooled those idiots, that pompous ginger cat, the silly Persian and the rest — I have it! I'll keep you around for a while.' He bit the mouse behind the ears. 'You can keep on scaring them, on my orders.'

'As you wish,' said the mouse, playing for time though he knew his was now short. And he told himself, 'One last effort for my race.'

At nine o'clock that evening a screaming hysterical albino cat was returned to the home. His eyes were leaping from his head and he cried, 'Such a dog! It had three heads — one a timber-wolf's, the middle one a mastiff's, and the other an Irish wolfhound's! It had two mouths on each head and three rows of teeth and —'

'Extr'ordinary performance!' said the ginger cat.

'Look where his psychology has got him,' said the tortoiseshell.

The Smart Dog

There was once a dog who discovered that he could talk, but he didn't lose his head. It happened when he was gnawing a bone on the dining-room carpet. His master saw this and began complaining: 'How many times have I got to tell you not to eat on the carpet?'

'Ah, pull your head in,' said the dog. 'It's about time you got rid of this old carpet.'

When he realized that he had spoken the dog turned tail and bolted.

'Don't you answer me back!' snapped his master after the dog.

The dog came back hastily.

'Excuse me, but I forgot this,' he said, snaffling the bone and bolting outside again.

As soon as he was outside the dog was very worried. He thought: That's torn it! As soon as that mug inside wakes up and realizes that I can talk, he'll lead me a man's life. I can kiss my old carefree life good-bye. Every evening and two afternoons a week I'll be on the halls. The only thing to do is to scram!

So he did, just in time, because the 'mug' came rushing out with his eyes as big as oranges, and calling after the dog: 'Hey, stop! I want to talk to you!'

'Not on your life!' said the dog, and kept on going. His master hailed a cab and after a few minutes he drew level with the dog.

'Stop and talk this over,' he pleaded. 'We can both make our fortunes.'

The dog galloped a little faster, and then replied over his shoulder: 'And spend all my life working as hard as a film star? I'm happy as I am.'

The cabby was so shocked at hearing a dog speak he ran his cab up on the footpath, and after the cabby and the dog's master had smoothed out three old ladies, the dog was half a mile ahead. When they drew level again the master said: 'One performance a week. I promise!'

'I know all about your promises,' panted the dog.

The man tried another approach.

'Towser! Come to heel! Come to heel!'

'I'm finished with that snuff!' said the dog, and doubled up a lane where the cab couldn't follow.

83

He'd gone about two hundred yards when a bag was flung over him, and when he was released he found himself with a dozen other dogs in a yard with a high fence. His new owner was a trainer in a circus.

'Just my luck!' said the dog. 'If this man discovers I can talk, I'm done for. I'll play dumb.'

And he did. He played so dumb that every day the trainer beat him because he wouldn't learn the simplest tricks. After a week of this the dog lost his temper.

'You hit me again and I'll bite you!' he snapped at the trainer.

The trainer dropped his stick.

'A miracle!' he shouted. 'My fortune is made. A talking dog at last, though I always reckoned I was on the verge of achieving it.'

He rushed in to embrace the dog, which was still angry and shouted back: 'Keep your smelly hands off me, you big ape!'

'Smelly, are they?' cried the trainer. 'Ah, well, I'll let it pass. What else do you think about me?'

'I could go on for five minutes,' said the dog, and began. But at the end of three minutes he realized he had fallen into a trap, and suddenly shut up and wouldn't say any more.

The trainer fell to beating him again after a time, but the dog remained silent under all the blows, and in the end the trainer gave up and went away.

'I ought to kick myself,' said the dog. 'I'm a goner unless I can think of something.'

Next morning the trainer was all smiles and love when he returned.

'I'm sorry I lost my temper, but the shock, you know, at hearing you speak —'

'Forget it,' said the dog.

'If there's anything I can do,' said the trainer. 'Just anything.'

'I don't think there is anything,' said the dog. 'Unless — unless —'

'Yes?' said the trainer eagerly.

'It's nothing much, but I wonder if I might be moved near the lions?' said the dog. 'It may sound odd, but I have always wanted to make a study of the king of beasts.'

It was done immediately, and for the rest of the day, apart from amiable conversations with the trainer, the dog gazed contemplatively at a very large and bad-tempered lion.

The next morning the trainer was again all love and smiles, but the dog refused to speak. After half an hour of futile arguments he would again have beaten the dog if his hand hadn't been stayed by hearing a voice from the lion's cage saying: 'Why the devil do you want to waste your time on a talking dog? There's nothing very remarkable about it. Everyone says dogs almost talk, so I ask you!'

The trainer was so startled he dropped his stick.

'You, too?' he gasped.

'Why not?'

The trainer went over to the lion's cage, and the lion began growling.

'Don't take any notice of my growls. Sometimes I get confused with my two voices, but I'll improve.'

'Well, I'll be —'

'Come closer,' said the lion, 'so that I can whisper. I don't want the dog to hear this.'

The trainer did so, and the lion killed him with a fearful smack of his huge paw.

Soon afterwards the little dog escaped. But never again did he speak. And as for telling anybody that he was a ventriloquist — well, who'd believe him?

John and the Blacksnake

One time John went down to the pond to catch him a few catfish. He put his line in the water, and cause the sun was warm John began to doze off a little. Soon as his head went down a little, he heard someone callin' his name, 'John, John,' like that. John jerked up his head and looked around, but he didn't see no one. Two-three minutes after that he heard it again, 'John, John.' He looked to one side and the other. He looked down at the water and he looked up in the air. And after that he looked behind him and saw a big old blacksnake settin' on a stone pile.

'Who been callin' my name?' says John.

'Me,' the blacksnake tell him. 'It's me that called you.'

John don't feel too comfortable talkin' to a blacksnake, and he feel mighty uneasy about a blacksnake talkin' to him. He say, 'What you want?'

'Just called your name to be sociable,' blacksnake tell him.

John look all around to see was anyone else there. 'How come you pick *me* to socialize with?'

'Well,' blacksnake say, 'you is the only one here, and besides that, John, ain't we both black?'

'Let's get it straight,' says John, 'they's two kinds of black, yours and mine, and they ain't the same thing.'

'Black is black,' blacksnake say, 'and I been thinkin' on it quite a while. You might say as we is kin.'

That was too much for John. He jumped up and sold out, went down the road like the Cannonball Express. And comin' down the road they was a wagon with Old Boss in it. Old Boss stop and wait till John get there. He say, 'John, I thought you was down to the pond fishin' for catfish?'

John looked back over his shoulder, said, 'I was, but I ain't.'

Old Boss say, 'John, you look mighty scared. What's your hurry?'

John say, 'Old Boss, when blacksnakes get to talkin', that's when I get to movin'.'

'Now, John,' Old Boss say, 'you know that blacksnakes don't talk.'

'Indeed I know it,' John say, 'and that's why, in

particular, I'm agoin', cause this here blacksnake is doin' what you say he don't.'

''Pears to me as you been into that corn liquor again,' Old Boss say. 'I'm disappointed in you, John. You let me down.'

'It ain't no corn liquor,' John say, 'it's worse than corn liquor. It's a big old blacksnake settin' on a rock pile down by the pond.'

'Well,' Old Boss say, 'let's go take a look.'

So Old Boss went with John back to the pond, and the blacksnake was still there settin' on the stones.

'Tell him,' John said to the blacksnake. 'Tell Old Boss what you told me.'

But the blacksnake just set there and didn't say a word.'

'Just speak up,' John say, 'tell him what I hear before.'

Blacksnake didn't have a word to say, and Old Boss tell John, 'John, you got to stay off that corn. I'm mighty disappointed in you. You sure let me down.' After that Old Boss got in his wagon and took off.

John looked mean at the blacksnake. He say, 'Blacksnake, how come you make me a liar?'

Blacksnake say, 'John, you sure let *me* down too. I spoke with you and nobody else. And the first thing you do is go off and tell everything you know to a white man.'

VIII

The Old Lady   88
Jonah and the Whale   90
The Lady and the Cowboy   92
Morris   94
Old Master and Okra   96
Noodle bug   100

The Old Lady

This is the story of a small sailing ship en route from San Francisco to Anchorage, Alaska. There were gales and high seas all the way, but eventually a terrible storm blew up. Against this alone the ship was helpless but a new danger soon appeared: a monstrous fish half as big again as the ship itself. It rammed the ship with its nose, lashed it with its tail, heaved it about on its back. It was clear the ship could not survive for long.

The captain and crew decided to throw their cargo overboard. Apart from making the ship more manageable they hoped that the oranges, which almost filled their holds, would be taken by the fish, which would then leave them alone. Indeed, as fast as they could throw the crates overboard the monster gulped them down. They served only to make it more angry and as the storm also increased in fury the more superstitious among the sailors began to believe that the monster itself was causing the storm. It had to be appeased and oranges, clearly, were not enough.

They drew lots. One man lost. They threw him overboard. The monster gulped him down and the storm continued but not, perhaps, quite as fiercely as before. It was difficult to tell. Another ballot and one more man went over the side, but he made little difference either to the storm or to the behaviour of the fish.

Now there was an old lady among the passengers: white hair, goldrimmed spectacles, red cheeks, knitting, rocking chair. Well, yes, a rocking chair. She had brought it with her and used to sit out on the deck before the storm got too bad. She reminded the crew of home and mother, so when she suggested that they threw her to the fish instead of sacrificing more members of the crew they immediately heaved her overboard, gold-rimmed spectacles, knitting, and rocking chair included.

The monster swallowed this latest offering and turned tail. The storm subsided. The crew set about repairing the ship and working out just where they were. Then they sailed on to Alaska.

When at last the ship reached port some weeks later the crew were greeted with the news that a monstrous fish had just been washed ashore. Naturally they went along to have a look and, yes, it was the same creature that had attacked them so viciously during the storm. How did they know? Well, when they cut it open there inside was the little old lady, rocking backwards and forwards in her rocking chair and selling the oranges to the sailors.

Jonah and the Whale

Well, to start with
It was dark
So dark
You couldn't see
Your hand in front of your face;
And huge
Huge as an acre of farm-land.
How do I know?
Well, I paced it out
Length and breadth
That's how.
And if you was to shout
You'd hear your own voice resound,
Bouncing along the ridges of its stomach,
Like when you call out
Under a bridge
Or in an empty hall.
Hear anything?
No not much,
Only the normal
Kind of sounds
You'd expect to hear
Inside a whale's stomach;
The sea swishing far away,
Food gurgling, the wind
and suchlike sounds;
Then there was me screaming for help,
But who'd be likely to hear,
Us being miles from
Any shipping lines
And anyway
Supposing someone did hear,
Who'd think of looking inside a whale?
That's not the sort of thing
That people do.
Smell? I'll say there was a smell.
And cold. The wind blew in
Something terrible from the South
Each time he opened his mouth
Or took a swallow of some tit bit.
The only way I found

To keep alive at all
Was to wrap my arms
Tight around myself
And race from wall to wall.
Damp? You can say that again;
When the ocean came sluicing in
I had to climb his ribs
To save myself from drowning.
Fibs? You think I'm telling you fibs,
I haven't told the half of it, brother.
I'm only giving a modest account
Of what these two eyes have seen
And that's the truth on it.
Here, one thing I'll say
Before I'm done —
Catch me eating fish
From now on.

The Lady and The Cowboy

Fred Stimson, of the Bar-U Cattle Company, was one of the West's most picturesque characters. He was a distinguished-looking man and no one would take him for anything but a gentleman no matter how rough, worn or soiled his clothing.

In the year 1887, Fred Stimson was in London during the celebrations connected with Queen Victoria's Jubilee. Stories regarding royalty were always of great interest to the cowpunchers and one cold, stormy night they asked for a story about the Jubilee. Fred did not need to be urged.

'Well, boys,' he began, 'on my arrival in London I went straight to the Hotel Cecil and had scarcely more than got nicely settled in my quarters when a bellhop came and said that I was wanted on the telephone. I went at once to the booth and took up the receiver. A sweet-voiced woman said, "Is that Mr Fred Stimson of High River, Alberta, Canada?" to which I replied that my name and address were quite correct. I nearly dropped dead with surprise when I was next informed that it was Queen Victoria speaking. I was so flabbergasted that I could only say: "Oh, your Majesty! I have often heard of you." But she put me quite at ease by saying, "And I have very often been informed of you and your doings in the far West, Mr Stimson. I hear that you are stopping at the Cecil?"

' "Yes, your Majesty," I replied, "and I am very comfortable."

' "No doubt you are, Mr Stimson, but I should like you to visit us at Buckingham Palace, and as we have rooms to burn here, I shall send the carriage for you."

'With this she rang off. I knew, of course, that a royal invitation was a command and I had scarcely got my traps together when I chanced to look out of the window. My heart nearly stopped beating when I saw the royal coach drawn by four white horses with outriders and postilions standing in front of the hotel. You should just have seen the flunkies of the Cecil dance attendance on me — they took me for some pumpkins, I can tell you. We drove at once to Buckingham Palace, and who should we meet at the door but Queen Victoria herself. She told off a couple of servants in livery to convey my luggage to a suite of rooms reserved for me. You ought to have seen the wonderful paintings, and Oriental rugs that you sank into when you walked on them, and a bed with a canopy over it and all of the other gorgeous things that you see in a palace. Well, boys, it was all very fine for a time, but after a while it began to pall on me so I went down town to see the sights and, falling in with some Canadian visitors in London, I stayed out pretty late. Next morning at breakfast the Queen, who had come to know me pretty well by this time, said, "Fred, you were a little late in getting home last night."

' "Yes, your Majesty," I said, "I met in with some western friends and —" but she cut me short with "Oh yes, I understand, boys will be boys, but for your convenience I shall see that you are supplied with a latchkey."

'Well, I received the key and carried it about with me, but a few evenings later, when strolling down Piccadilly, I ran into a bunch of Alberta boys and we made a night of it. I got back to Buckingham Palace at about 3 a.m. and fiddled around with the latchkey for a time. Presently I heard a window overhead go up and a soft voice called out, "Is that you, Fred?" Recognizing it at once as that of the Queen, I replied, "It is, your Majesty, I have the latchkey all right, but I can't find the keyhole." "Never mind," said she, "just wait until I put on my crown and I'll come down and let you in." And sure enough she did.'

Morris

Morris is walking along Seventh Avenue with his friend Abe, and they keep walking along the street and Morris calls, 'Hello, Joe. Hello, Sam. Hello, Max. Hello, Jim. Hello, Bob. Hello, Garry. Hello, Frank.'

And Abe asks, 'Morris, what is this with you? What? You know all these people?'

He says, 'Of course. They're all personal friends of mine. Look, my name is Morris. I know everybody.'

Abe says, 'Morris, don't give me that stuff. I'm a friend of yours. What do you tell me you know everybody? Maybe you know the Mayor?

He says, 'Ed? Ed is my best friend. I had lunch with him the other day.'

Abe says, 'I don't believe you.'

'Come into the phone booth. I'll call him up and invite him to say hello to you.'

So he gets on the phone.

'I'd like to speak to Ed Koch.'

'Who's calling?'

'Morris.'

'Hello, Morris! How are you? What can I do for you?'

'I've got a friend of mine here. He doesn't believe I know you. Will you say hello to him?'

He says hello.

'Gee, Morris, that's amazing! Do you mean to tell me — I can't believe you know everybody. Maybe you know the — the — the Governor?'

He says, 'The Governor? Mario? My bosom buddy! My wife and his wife went to the beauty parlour together the other day. Fact is, we've got dinner with them Friday night.'

Abe says, 'Don't give me that stuff!'

'I'll call him over the phone.'

He gets Albany on the phone and he says, 'I want you to say hello to a friend of mine.'

Sure enough, Mario Guomo!

Abe says, 'Maybe you're such a *knacker* — maybe you know the President?'

'Do I know the President? Ronnie? Ronnie's my bosom buddy. We're talking to each other four times a week.'

Abe says, 'Don't give me that stuff!'

'So, I'll call him up.'

So he calls him up, and sure enough Morris knows Ronnie and Ronnie knows Morris. Ronnie says hello to Abe.

Abe says, 'Look, Morris, don't give me that baloney you know everybody in the world. I know somebody you don't know.'

'Please, this is Morris you're talking to. I know everybody.'

So Abe says, 'I'll tell you what. I'll make you a bet that you don't know the Pope.'

So he says, 'Look, my name's Morris. I know the Pope — guaranteed. I'll tell you what we'll do. We'll take a trip to Rome. If I don't know the Pope, I'll pay. If I know him, you'll pay for the trip.'

'Fair enough.'

So they go to Rome and sure enough they watch. The Pope comes out on the balcony every day at twelve o'clock, and he waves to the crowd in the piazza.

So Morris says, 'You see, jerk. Tomorrow at twelve o'clock the Pope's going to come out there and I'm going to come out with him on the balcony, just to show you that I know him.'

So Abe says, 'Sure, sure.'

So the next day comes around. Abe is waiting in the piazza and suddenly twelve o'clock rolls around and out comes the Pope. Morris got his arm around him and the Pope's got his arm around Morris. So Abe's looking up there and he's dumfounded. All of a sudden a little Italian kid comes by and he pulls him by the leg and he says, 'Hey, mister, who's the guy up there with Morris?'

Old Master and Okra

Old Master had to go down to New Orleans on business, and he left his number-one slave named Okra in charge of things. Okra declared to himself he goin' to have a good time whilst Old Master was away, and the thing he did the very first mornin' was to go out and tell the other slaves, 'Now you get on with your affairs. Old Master gone to New Orleans and we got to keep things goin'.'

Then Okra went in the kitchen to cook himself up some food, and in the process of doin' so he got ruffled and spilled the bacon grease on top of the stove. It burst up into a big fire, and the next thing you know that house was goin' up in flame and smoke. Okra he went out the window and stood off a ways.

lookin' real sorry. By the time the other hands got there, wasn't nothin' else to do *but* look sorry. They was so busy with lookin' that they never noticed that the sparks lit in the wood lot and set it afire too. Well, Okra ordered everybody out to the wood lot to save it, but by then the grass was sizzlin' and poppin', a regular old prairie fire roarin' across the fields, burnin' up the cotton and everything else. They run over there with wet bags to beat it out, but next thing they knowed, the pasture was afire and all Old Master's cattle was a-goin' throttle out and racin' for the Texas Badlands.

Okra went to the barn for the horses, but soon's he opened the door they bolted and was gone. 'If'n I can get that ox team hitched,' Okra said, 'I'll go on down to Colonel Thatcher's place and get some help.' Well, minute he started to put the yoke on them oxen, the left-hand ox lit out and was gone. The right-hand ox went after him, and the both of 'em just left Okra holdin' the ox yoke up in the air. When Old Master's huntin' dog see them oxen go off that way, he figured something was wrong, and he sold out, barkin' and snappin' at their heels.

'Bout that time Okra looked around and found all the slaves had took off, too, headin' North and leavin' no tracks. He was all alone, and he had to digest all that misery by himself.

Week or two went by, and Okra went down to meet the boat Old Master comin' back on. Old Master got off feelin' pretty good. Told Okra to carry his stuff and say, 'Well, Okra, how'd things go while I was away?'

'Fine, just fine,' Okra say. 'I notice they're fixin' the bridge over Black Creek. Ain't that good?'

'Yeah,' Old Master say, 'that's fine, Okra, just fine. Soon's we get home I'm goin' to change my clothes and do some quail shootin'.'

'Captain,' Okra say, hangin' his head, 'I got a little bad news for you.'

'What's that?' Old Master say.

'You ain't neither goin' quail huntin',' Okra say, 'your huntin' dog run away.'

Old Master took it pretty good. He say, 'Well, don't worry about it none, he'll come back. How'd he happen to run away?'

'Chasin' after the right-hand ox,' Okra say. 'That ox just lit out one mornin'.'

'Where to?' Old Master say.

'I don't know where to,' Okra say. 'He was tryin' to catch up with the left-hand ox.'

Old Master began to frown now, and he say to Okra, 'You mean the whole ox team is gone? How come?'

'I was yokin' 'em up to go after Colonel Thatcher, after the horses bolted,' Okra say.

'How come the horses bolted?' Old Boss say.

'Smoke from the pasture grass. That's what scared all your livestock and made 'em break down the fence and run for the swamp.'

'You mean all my livestock is gone? Okra, I goin' to skin you. How'd that pasture get on fire?'

Okra he just stood there lookin' foolish, scratchin' his head. 'Reckon the fire just came across from the cotton field, Captain,' he say.

'You mean my cotton's burned!' Old Master holler. 'How'd that happen?'

'Couldn't put it out, Captain. Soon as we see it come over there from the wood lot, we went down with wet bags but we couldn't handle it. Man, that was sure a pretty cotton field before the fire got there.'

Right now Old Master was lookin' pretty sick. He talk kind of weak. 'Okra, you tryin' to tell me the wood lot's gone too?'

'I hate to tell you, Captain, but you guessed it,' Okra say, kind of sad. 'Imagine, all them trees gone, just 'cause of one lonesome spark.'

Old Master couldn't hardly talk at all now. He just whisperin'. 'Okra,' he say, 'Okra, where'd that spark come from?'

'Wind blew it right from the house,' Okra say, 'it was when the big timbers gave and came down. Man, sparks flew in the air a mile or more.'

'You mean the house burned up?' Old Master say.

'Oh, yeah, didn't I tell you?' Okra reply. 'Didn't burn *up*, though, so much as it burned *down*.'

By now Old Master was a miserable sight, pale as a ghost and shakin' all over.

'Okra, Okra,' Old Master say, 'let's go get the field hands together and do somethin'!'

'Can't do that,' Okra say, 'I forget to tell you, they's all sold out for Michigan.'

Old Master just set there shakin' his head back and forth. 'Okra,' he say, 'why didn't you come right out with it? Why you tell me everything was fine?'

'Captain, I'm sorry if I didn't tell it right,' Okra say. 'Just wanted to break it to you easy.'

Noodle bug

One bright Thursday morning
P.C. Plod was on pointduty in Williamson Square
when he was approached by an oriental gentleman,
new to the city, who wanted to know
the whereabouts of a certain Chinese restaurant.
To Plod, one Chinese restaurant was as good,
or as bad, as another, and so he
directed the old man to the nearest.

Ten minutes later, the old man returned:
'Please could you dilect me to Yuet Ben Lestaurant'
'That's a coincidence' remarked Plod
'You're the second Chinaman to ask me that in ten
    minutes,
is there a party on?'
'Me same Chinaman,' explained the same Chinaman.
To cover up his embarrassment,
Plod gave detailed directions
of a restaurant on the far side of the city.
The old man trundled off.

Twenty minutes later, tired and angry,
he was back in Williamson Square.
Lest a member of our Police Force be thought
less than wonderful and idiotic to boot,
Plod sought immediately to pacify
the stranger with polite conversation.
'Now then sir what have you there in that large bag
that weighs so heavily upon you?'
'In bag there is special Chinese flour'
'And what's that used for sir?'
persisted the trafficcontrolling seeker
of eternal truth and wisdom.
'Ah well, special flour is mixed with water until
velly soft and then whole family arrive for
ceremony and everybody pull and roll and pull
and roll and pull and roll until we have big soft
noodle six foot in length'
'Garn, silliest thing I ever heard' scoffed Plod
'What could you do with a big soft noodle six foot
    long?'
'You could put it on pointduty in Williamson Square'
suggested the old man and
                    ran

                        off

                            down

                                the

                                      page

**When he was born he was so big we
couldn't name all of him at once.**

IX

Jack and the Devil 102
Jim Buckey, Strong Man 104
The Fast Fencers 104
Crooked Mick goes for a Job 106
The Sissy from Anaconda 110

Jack and the Devil

Jack and the Devil wuz settin' down under a tree one day arguin' 'bout who was the strongest. The Devil got tired of talkin' and went and picked up a mule. Jack went and picked up the same mule. The Devil run to a great big old oak tree and pulled it up by the roots. Jack grabbed holt of one jus' as big and pulled it up. The Devil broke a anchor cable. Jack took it and broke it agin.

So the Devil says, 'Shucks! This ain't no sho nuff trial. This is chillun foolishness. Meet me out in that hund'ed acre clearin' tomorrow mornin' at nine o'clock and we'll see who kin throw my hammer the furtherest. The one do that is the strongest.'

Jack says, 'That suits me.'

So nex' mawnin' the Devil wuz there on time wid his hammer. It wuz bigger'n the white folks church house in Winter Park. A whole heap uh folks had done come out tuh see which one would win.

Jack wuz late. He come gallopin' up on hawseback and reined in the hawse to short till he reared up his hind legs.

Jack jumped off and says: 'Wese all heah, le's go. Who goin' first?'

The Devil tole 'im, 'Me. Everybody stand back and gimme room.'

So he throwed the hammer and it went so high till it went clean outa sight. Devil tole 'em, 'Iss Tuesday now. Y'all go home and come back Thursday mornin' at nine. It won't fall till then.'

Sho 'nuff the hammer fell on Thursday mornin' at nine o'clock and knocked out a hole big as Polk County.

They lifted the hammer out the hole and levelled it and it wuz Jack's time to throw.

Jack took his time and walked 'round the hammer to the handle and took holt of it and throwed his head back and looked up at the sky.

'Look out, Rayfield! Move over, Gabriel! You better stand 'way back, Jesus! I'm fixin' to throw.' He meant Heaven.

Devil run up to 'im, says, 'Hold on there a minute! Don't you throw my damn hammer up there! I left a whole lot uh my tools up there when they put me out and I ain't got 'em back yet. Don't you *throw* my hammer up there!'

It was so windy one year Good Friday didn't arrive until Easter Sunday and Witsun didn't make it at all.

Jim Buckey, Strong Man

When I was punching cows out in the Twenty Mile district, I rode out acrosst that prairie stretch from the ranch house, and I was about twelve miles out when that horse of mine — which was half Hamilton and half Kentucky, full of timothy hay and lots of oats, started to gallop till he got really out of control, when the blankety-blank beast ran his foot in a prairie-dog hole. And going as fast as we were, he naturally just broke his leg and rolled over so damn quick I couldn't get away from him, and he pinned my foot under him. And there I was twelve miles from the ranch. I had to walk clear back to the ranch to get a pole off the corral fence to pry that damn horse off my foot. Those were the kind of days you tenderfoots don't know anything about.

The Fast Fencers

In the days when a lot of fencing was being done in the outback, a traveller passing through a town in western Queensland decided to stay at the local hostelry for the night.

Equipping himself with a pot of beer, the stranger drifted out on the front verandah, where a number of drinkers were squatting in earnest conversation.

It was the usual bush talk — in this instance, an argument as to who, among the locals, was the best and fastest fencer.

Someone said, 'I reckon Dan O'Brien'd take some beating. He can put up eighty posts a day.'

'What about Rusty Curry?' said another. 'He can do ninety!'

A third man snorted and claimed that Harry Townsend could erect a hundred posts in a day.

The talk began to lag a little and the stranger was thinking of going indoors for another pot when an old-timer piped up: 'Those blokes you mentioned are a bunch of unweaned amateurs. Why, I recall the Gray brothers — Tom and Harry. Used to take three days' tucker with 'em every morning when they went out on a fencing job.'

The stranger, who had grown interested, couldn't help asking, 'Why did they take three days' tucker with them if they were only going out for the day?'

The old-timer spat thoughtfully in the sand.

'Because,' he said quietly, 'every time they did a day's fencing they worked so fast that it took them two days to get back.'

In one week Irish Paddy dug so many post-holes it took him a fortnight to walk back to where he'd started from.

Crooked Mick goes for a Job

Shortly after he had come of age, Crooked Mick decided to apply for a job as a shearer on Speewah Station.

'I dunno,' said the Boss. 'You look strong enough, Mick, but shearing requires brains as well as stamina. I'll have to test your ability before I put you on.'

'Right-o,' agreed Mick. 'What do I have to do?'

'Well, I'm not getting enough power out of that windmill that pumps bore water into the homestead dam. See what you can do to step up the flow.'

Mick thought deeply for a while. Then he happened to see a willy-willy whirlwind racing across one of the mustering paddocks. He tore off after it and caught up with it near Bundaberg as it was getting ready to move out to sea. For more than an hour Mick wrestled with the willy-willy and when he had finally subdued it he compressed it like a concertina and carried it carefully back to the homestead dam.

Mick harnessed the willy-willy to the windmill and called the Boss over to see the increase in power. But unfortunately, Mick had fitted in the willy-willy wrong way round. It acted in reverse; and while the Boss watched with paralysed horror the windmill sucked every drop of water out of the dam and sent it back into the bowels of the earth where it had come from.

'Sorry, Mick,' said the Boss, 'but I can't take you on. You'd never make the grade as a shearer.'

Crooked Mick pleaded for a fair go. And after a while the Boss relented and said, 'Well, I'll give you one more chance. There's a mob of old wethers in the far paddock, that has to be rendered down into tallow. I'll leave you to look after the job.'

Mick tended the boiling-down works, and everything went well for a month or so. Then one unlucky day, while he was stirring a vat full of molten dripping, he slipped and fell head-first into the bubbling depths.

Some station hands heard Mick's cry as he disappeared into the vat. They hurried over and pulled him out by his feet, which hadn't been quite submerged. They tore the clothing off him; and one fast-thinking man slapped a freshly skinned fleece, still warm, around the unfortunate Mick's body. There was no time to lose. Quickly harnessing the station gig, two of the hands set off with the fleece-covered victim on the 550-mile trip to the nearest medical aid.

The men stood anxiously outside the surgery while the doctor battled for the life of Crooked Mick. At last the medico came out and said with a sad shake of his head, 'I've done my best, boys, but I'm afraid I got him a little too late.'

'Stiffen the wombats!' gasped one of the station hands, 'we didn't think he'd peg out!'

'Oh, he won't die,' the doctor assured them. 'What I meant was that the warm fleece, meeting the raw, hot skin, took graft and has started to grow. He'll have that fleece for as long as he lives.'

Each year, after that, they rounded Crooked Mick up for shearing. He yielded a pretty fair clip, too — twenty-two pounds of wool, according to the old-timers.

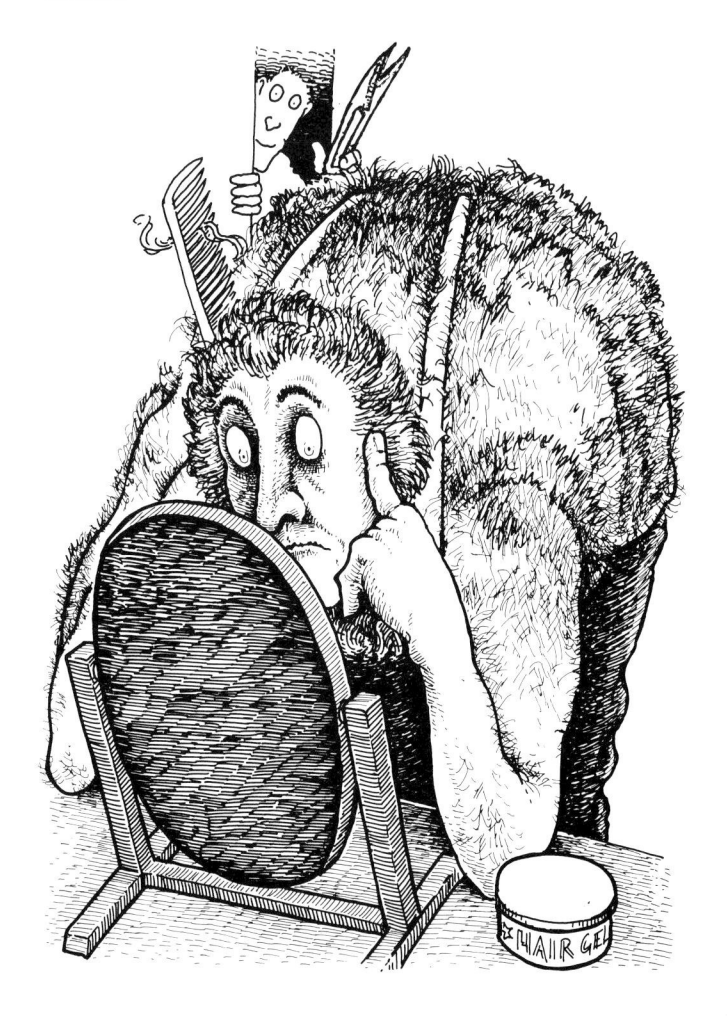

When Mick had recovered from this ordeal and was on his feet again, he went to the Boss and said, 'Well, how about the shearin' job?'

'I couldn't take you on, Mick,' growled the Boss. 'You're too bloody careless.'

Well, Crooked Mick pleaded for a fair go. So the Boss stroked his chin, and pushed his hat back on his head, and said to Mick, 'I'll give you one more chance, and this is positively the last. There's mobs of dingoes coming round the sheep after dark. We used to be able to shoot a few every time we went out, but for some reason unbeknowns to us we never catch one of them, these nights. Find out what's making them so hard to hit.'

'Right-o,' said Mick.

Arming himself with a shotgun and ammunition he set out that night for a spot some distance from where one of the largest mobs of sheep was quietly grazing. He built a fire and then sat down to wait. An hour passed, and another, and then Mick saw, just beyond the circle of light cast by the camp-fire, about three or four hundred pairs of eyes watching him. He blasted away with his shotgun, aiming always between the eyes, and presently there wasn't a dingo to be seen. They'd either been killed or had fled. Mick decided to wait until morning to see the size of his catch.

But when the dawn light came, Crooked Mick's surprise was exceeded only by his annoyance. For there wasn't a dead dingo anywhere in sight.

Mick knew that his marksmanship was second to none in the whole of the Speewah territory. So next night he went back to the spot where he had camped previously; and this time he took along with him the Number One Nitkeeper of the Speewah Two-Up School. This bloke was so sharp-eyed he could have tracked a sandfly across Sturt's Stony Desert. They built a big fire; and while Mick sat beside it, his mate climbed up into a nearby tree.

They hadn't long to wait. Out of the darkness came some 200 dingoes. They circled the fire at a distance, their eyes glowing. Mick fired at them, aiming between their eyes. They seemed to linger for a while, and then dispersed.

The nitkeeper came down out of the tree. 'Well, stone the lizards!' he said, an unbelieving look in his eyes, 'you won't believe this, Mick, but them dingoes came along in pairs, and each beast had its outer eye closed — so that when you aimed at a point half-way between their eyes *you was actually shooting between the two animals*. Talk about clever!'

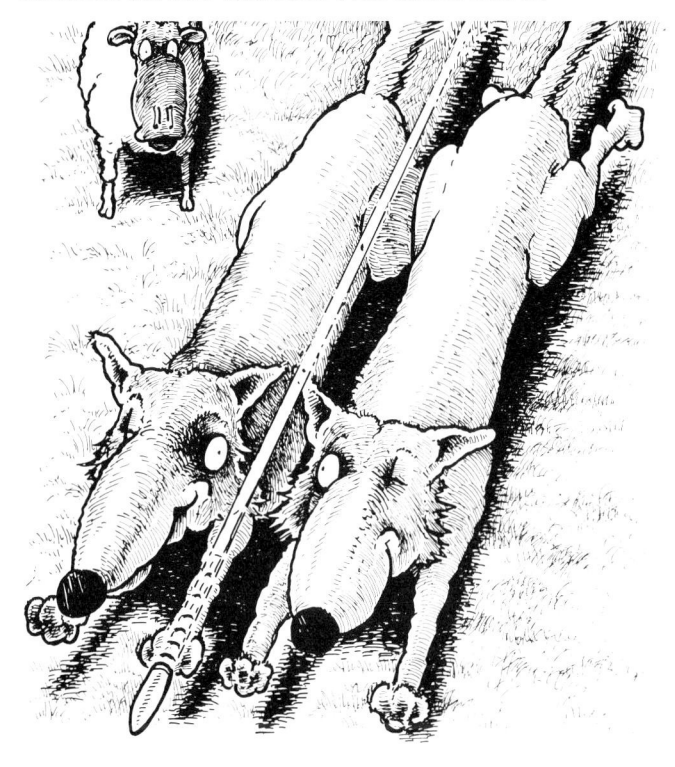

This information satisfied Crooked Mick. He had learned the secret of the Speewah dingoes. When they came padding round his camp-fire on the following night he was able, by careful aiming, to shoot the whole mob.

When Mick handed a pile of some 200 scalps to the Boss, he was so impressed that he said, 'All right, Mick, you win. Get your blades and start in the shearing shed next Monday. But it's only for a trial, mind you. If you're no good I'll have to sack you.'

Well, as everybody knows, Crooked Mick became the ringer of the Speewah shed; and if the old-timers are to be believed nobody has ever beaten his tally of 1,847 wethers and twelve lambs shorn in one day with the blades.

It's so hot in Yuma people are buried in their overcoats so that they don't freeze when they get to Hell.

The Sissy from Anaconda

The old bartender at the Exchange Saloon knew more about early Butte than anybody else. He said to a visitor, 'Well, mister, so you heard Butte is tough. I tell you Butte is not tough. But we had a tough town right near here. Did you ever hear of Anaconda?' And the old bartender recited his story as follows:

It was 20-odd years ago, one hot day in August, and there was a bunch of us sittin' out on the porch here, when we see comin' down the trail a little old man. He was leadin' a great big cougar in one hand and a grizzly bear in the other. They were both on leashes.

When he got in front of the saloon, he stopped and reached over and took that cougar by the ears and slammed him down on his haunches and said: 'Sit there, you hear?'

Then he turned around and looked at the bear. And when the bear started to whine, he spit in the bear's eye and said, 'Shut up.'

The little old guy then walked into the saloon, lookin neither left nor right, and went up to the bar and said, 'Give me a bottle of your best drinkin' liquor.'

I set out a bottle on the counter — and a tumbler. He looked at the tumbler and looked up at me, took the tumbler and threw it down to the floor — broke it to pieces. Then he up with the liquor and drank it straight down. Gurgle, gurgle! Thirty-two ounces. Down she went in the hatch in two big drinks.

He put it back on the counter, the empty bottle, wiped his lips with his sleeve, and said, 'Well, mister, that was pretty good. Now give me another glass of that wine.'

So I put out another bottle. He up with it and was just goin to start a-drinkin', then he stopped. He set it down on the counter and began fumblin', reachin' into his shirt, as if searchin' for something.

And then, mister, he pulled out the damndest rattlesnake I ever see!

There was fourteen rattles on it and they was all clackin' like castanets. And that snake's mouth was open and drippin' with venom.

The little guy looked at him and said: 'Ugh! I'll learn you to bite me, you . . .!' And he bit off the rattlesnake's head and spit it out, then drank up the liquor.

I said: 'Say, mister, where do you come from?'

The little guy says: 'Who me?'

And I said: 'Yes, where do *you* come from?'

'Oh,' he says, 'I come from down the road a piece here. A town called Anaconda.'

'Oh,' I said, 'so you come from Anaconda, do you?'

'Yep.'

'Well,' I said, 'they must be pretty tough down there.'

'Tough,' he said. 'Hell! They run all of us sissies out of there yesterday!'

The water's so hard you have to chop it with an axe.

X

The Hickory Toothpick   112
The Year of the Big Freeze   114
Hot   116
Water in the Gourd   118

The Hickory Toothpick

One winter we sure had a big snow. I was livin' up a ways on Pine Mountain, south side. And one morning I tried to open the door, but I couldn't. I'd noticed the snow banked up on the windows, but when I tried the door it looked like the snow had piled up plumb over the house.

I kept my stove goin'. Had me a fairly good pile of wood in the house — and enough rations for a day or two. But after about four days my wood was gone, and the meat, too. I tore out some shelves and kept my fire up. The snow didn't seem to thaw much, and after I'd burned up all my shelves and a couple of chairs I knew I had to get out of there and hunt me some firewood.

So I took the stovepipe down: knocked a few planks loose from around the flue, got my axe and crawled out. Well, the snow went up like a funnel, twenty or thirty feet, where my fire had kept it melted. So I hacked me some toeholds with the axe and finally made it out on top of all that snow. And like I said, it was a big snowfall: plumb over the tops of the tallest trees.

But 'way up on one cliff of Pine Mountain there was one tree — a hickory – the snow hadn't drifted over and buried. So I headed for it. The crust was hard enough to hold me and up I went.

Got to that hickory tree finally — and it was full of coons. That hickory was ripe with 'em: frozen fast asleep. So I says, 'Well, here's firewood, and meat too, to do me till a thaw sets in.' I shook the coons out and picked up about a dozen: tore a thin strip of bark off that hickory and tied 'em together by their tails.

Then I cut that tree. Went to trimmin' it. Piled up the limbs right careful, so's I'd have plenty of kindlin'. Oh, I saved every twig! But — don't you know! — when I hacked off that last limb, the log jumped and slid top foremost down the south side of the mountain. There went my stovewood!

I watched it slitherin' down, faster and faster. It was goin' so fast it shot across the bottom and up Black Mountain it flew. I thought it 'uld go right up in the air but it slowed down just at the top of the ridge: stopped with its top teeterin' — and here it came back. Scooted across where the river was and headed up The Pine again. I thought I'd catch it with the axe when it got to me, but when I tried to nail it, it was about four inches too short. Stopped right at me, and down again. Hit through the bottom goin' so fast it was smokin'. Up Black Mountain, clean to the top, and back down this way again. Well I watched it see-sawin' a few times, and finally gathered up my coons and that pile of brush and made it back to the house. Put the flue and stovepipe back and started my fire.

Well, I lived off coon-meat for about a week. Had to burn up all my chairs, and the table, to keep from freezin'. And I'd started burnin' the bedstead and was fryin' the last of my meat when I heard, drip! drip! drip! And there was a little daylight showin' at the top of the windows. So I shoved on the door, mashed the snow back and got out. Snow was still about eight foot deep. Got my axe and headed for the nearest tree. Got me a good pile of wood in and fixed the fire till my little stove was red-hot.

Had to go fetch some meal and other rations as I was gettin' a little hungry. So I took off for the store at Putney.

I looked over the country and noticed a sort of trough there between the two mountains where that log had been slidin'. I went right down there. Couldn't see that hickory at all. But when I got to the bottom of that trough I looked, and there — still slidin' back and forth just a few inches — was my log. And — don't you know! — with all that see-sawin' that log had worn down to the size of a toothpick. I leaned over and picked it up. Stuck it in my pocket.

You may not believe me, but—I've kept it to this day —There. Look at it yourself. Best toothpick I ever had.

The Year of the Big Freeze

The year of the big freeze, ice on the Rogue at Battle Bar was so thick cattle and horses crossed the river upon it. It turned cold so suddenly, some wild creatures were surprised. Scattered here and there were salmon lying on the ice which quickly froze under them when they jumped into the air for the purpose of discovering how they were progressing upon their journey to the creek of their nativity. A big blue heron pecked at a frog which was sitting upon a rock under the water, and before it could withdraw its bill the ice froze around it and held the bird fast. Hathaway Jones chopped the ice away from the heron's bill with an axe, and when it straightened up it still had the frog, which it swallowed.

Thin ice on standing water, which is common on frosty mornings, was all Hathaway had ever before seen. His grandfather, Ike, had told him of thick ice which forms on some eastern lakes and rivers: how the people skate, and drive wagon trains upon it. Testing the ice on the Rogue, he discovered it would support him, so he decided to take a walk.

He was having a grand time sliding around, and sometimes sitting down abruptly, never dreaming the ice might not be thick enough all along the river to stand his weight. Suddenly he broke through into the swift, cold water which carried him under the ice.

Swimming downstream with all his might in the hopes of seeing a hole in the ice through which he could crawl out, he was very glad he had practised holding his breath. It was cold under the ice, and his heavy clothing and shoes weighted him down to the bottom of the river. There he saw a big Chinook salmon and grabbed it by the tail, knowing it would, when scared, swim downstream.

The salmon darted away like an arrow from a long bow, towing Hathaway through the water so fast the friction warmed him. He enjoyed the speed and the warm glow which suffused him, but was at a loss to know how he would breathe after tiring of holding his breath.

Now Hathaway knew that salmon desiring to rid themselves of hooks or other undesirable obstacles usually leap high out of the water and shake their heads. He was thinking of that very thing when the fish whose tail he was holding saw a hole in the ice and leaped with all its strength. It was a big salmon, and a strong one. It leaped so high it landed upon the ice beyond the hole, dragging Hathaway out with it.

Whereupon he threw the salmon across his shoulders and carried it home for supper, helping himself along with a straight stick which he found by the trail. Arriving at the cabin, he leaned the stick against the wall back of the stove where the heat thawed it, and it turned out to be a snake.

They have nine months of winter out there. The rest of the time the ice is too thin to skate.

Hot

'It's sure hot around here.'

'Hot? How come you call this hot? It's pure cool to me. Down where I come from it's so hot you dassent leave your hammer in the sun, cause the heat takes the temper right out of it.'

'Hot? You call that hot? Why, down in the bottoms where my daddy lives all the fence posts bend over in the middle when the sun comes up, and the logs and stumps in the fields crawl away to find some shade.'

'Well, that sounds kind of *warm* all right, but it sure ain't hot. Down in my country when the dogs is chasin' cats down the main street they is all walkin'.'

'I forgot to tell you one more thing about my place. Was so hot down there that when we pumped water nothin' but steam come out. So we had to catch that steam and put it in the ice house at night to turn it back to water.'

'Speakin' of the ice house, we had to keep the popcorn there, else it popped right off the ears and covered the ground like snow.'

'Well, that ain't much to mention. Where I come from the railroad tracks set out there in the sun long as they can stand it, then they burrow under the ground and don't come out till dark. That's how come the train don't go through till midnight.'

'What you-all are talkin' about is plain cool to me. We got a creek down in my country that runs like the devil at night. But when the sun comes up in the morning this creek begins to get sluggish in the heat, and by ten o'clock it just stops in its tracks and don't move at all till the sun goes down.'

'We got a creek too down on my daddy's farm, and if you go out there in the middle of the day you hear all the stones hollerin' something pitiful for somebody to come quick and throw them in the water.'

'My mamma had a great big iron kettle, and she left it outside one time for just about ten minutes in the sun. And when she took it in it had great big water blisters on it.'

'That does it! When *my* mamma left her iron kettle in the sun it melted down flat and she had to use it for a stove lid.'

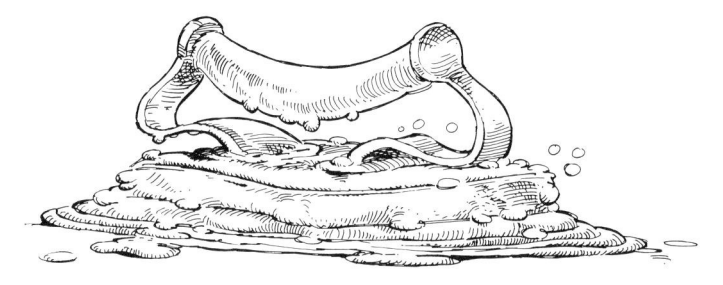

'Ain't you forget to hear about the big old swamp on my granddaddy's forty acres? When it gets hot there that swamp rises up like a cake till it's thirty feet high, and it don't go down till the frost hits.'

'The way it seem to me is where we're sittin' is just too cold, so somebody go and fetch my coat.'

It's so hot in Texas sometimes that the tree stumps crawl off to hide in the shade.

Water in the Gourd

Mas' Eddy was a small farmer. Each morning he rose very early to work on his land which lay five chains from his home. Before he left, his wife, Dulcimena, cooked him some yam and roasted breadfruit to take with him for his breakfast.

'Only fool man work on empty stomick,' she would say, 'make sure you stop to eat.'

Dulcimena also gave him a big gourd filled with water. Mas' Eddy was very proud of this gourd. It was a very big gourd that he had picked off a calabash tree near the sea one year.

One morning — it was a Tuesday — Mas' Eddy got up as usual to go to work in his field. First he tied his trousers above the ankle with string, then he filled his pockets with the yam and roasted breadfruit, slung the gourd of water over his shoulder and picked up his hoe and cutlass. He wrapped the handle of the cutlass in paper and put it on the top of his head. He always carried his cutlass that way.

On the way to his field he stopped a few times to chat with people on the road and so the sun had already risen when he got there. Mas' Eddy hung his gourd on the branch of a tree by its string and set to work right away. He worked very busily for a couple of hours, clearing the land with his cutlass, digging holes with his hoe, and planting some corn he had brought with him. The ants were particularly troublesome this year and he stopped from time to time to brush them off his trouser legs. By eleven o'clock in the morning he was hot and thirsty. He decided to stop for a drink of water and some breadfruit.

He went to the tree to get the gourd but to his astonishment it wasn't there.

'But how can it have gone?' muttered Mas' Eddy to himself, wrinkling his forehead. 'No one has been here but me. A duppy must have taken it.'

Duppies, as everyone knows, are fond of playing those kind of tricks on people.

He was just about to turn away in disappointment when he noticed something. The string, which had been tied round the neck of the gourd, was still hanging down from the tree. And it was hanging down very stiffly as though something heavy were on the end of it. Mas' Eddy went a little closer and took a good look. His eyes turned crossways and his grey hairs curled even tighter to his head. The ants had eaten away the gourd — all except a tiny piece of the neck held by the string — but the water was still hanging in mid-air.

Mas' Eddy walked round and round the tree but each time that he came back to the same place the water was still there. It was rounded in shape like the gourd and the sun glistened on its sides. The only problem was how Mas' Eddy was to drink it.

'If I try to pick it up in my hands,' he thought, 'my hands will simply go through the water. And if I untie the string the water may fall to the ground. I had better suck it up.'

So Mas' Eddy stood right underneath the water, pressed his lips to its side and sucked. The water slid down his hot, parched throat — cool, liquid, and sweet. He sucked and sucked until finally the string bobbed lightly up and down with no weight on the end of it at all. Mas' Eddy had drunk all the water.

And that of course was his big mistake. Obviously he should have left the water hanging there and called his neighbours to come and look at it. Because to this day no one believes that the ants ate up his gourd and left the water hanging by a string.

The only person who believes Mas' Eddy is his wife Dulcimena. Ask Dulcimena if it happened and she will reply with a shrug of her shoulders: 'Anything could happen to that fool man,' and go back to boiling her yams.

XI

Plenty Rations is Comin'   120
Crooked Mick the Hunter   123
Cougar Tamer   126
A Snake Yarn   127

Plenty Rations is Comin'

A man had a wife and a whole passle of young 'uns, and they didn't have nothin' to eat.

He told his ole lady, 'Well, I got a load of ammunition in my gun, so I'm gointer go out in the woods and see what I kin bring back for us to eat.'

His wife said: 'That's right, go see can't you kill us somethin' — if 'tain't nothin' but a squirrel.'

He went on huntin' wid his gun. It was one of these muzzle-loads. He knowed he didn't have but one load of ammunition so he was very careful not to stumble and let his run go off by accident.

He had done walked more'n three miles from home and he ain't saw anything to shoot at. He got worried. Then all of a sudden he spied some wild turkeys settin' up in a tree on a limb. He started to shoot at 'em, when he looked over in the pond and seen a passle of wild ducks; and down at the edge of the pond he saw a great big deer. He heard some noise behind him and he looked 'round and seen some partiges.

He wanted all of 'em and he didn't know how he could get 'em. So he stood and he thought and he thought. Then he decided what to do.

He took aim, but he didn't shoot at the turkeys. He shot the limb the turkeys was settin' on and the ball split that limb and let all them turkeys' feets dropped right down thru the crack and the split limb shet up on 'em and helt 'em right there. The ball went on over and fell into the pond and kilt all them ducks. The gun had too heavy a charge in her, so it burst and the barrel flew over and kilt that deer. The stock kicked the man in the breast and he fell backwards and smothered all them partiges.

Well, he drug his deer up under the tree and got his ducks out the pond and piled them up wid the turkeys and so forth. He seen he couldn't tote all that game so he went on home to git his mule and wagon.

Soon as he came in the gate his wife said:

'Where is the game you was gointer bring back? You musta lost yo' gun, you ain't got it.'

He told his wife, 'I wears the longest pants in this house. You leave me tend to my business and you mind yours. Jus' you put on the pot and be ready. Plenty rations is comin'.'

He took his team on back in the woods wid him and loaded up the wagon. He wouldn't git up on the wagon hisself because he figgered his mule had enough to pull without him.

Just as he got his game all loaded on the wagon, it commenced to rain but he walked on beside of the mule pattin' him and tellin' him to 'come up,' till they got home.

When he got home his wife says: 'The pot is boilin'. Where is the game you tole me about?'

He looked back and seen his wagon wasn't behind the mule where it ought to have been. Far as he could see — nothin' but them leather traces, but no wagon.

Then he knowed the rain had done made them traces stretch, and the wagon hadn't moved from where he loaded it.

So he told his wife, 'The game will be here. Don't you worry.'

So he just took the mule out and stabled him and wrapped them traces 'round the gate post and went on in the house.

The next day it was dry and the sun was hot and it shrunk up them traces, and about twelve o'clock they brought that wagon home, 'Cluck-cluck, cluck-cluck,' right on up to the gate.

Crooked Mick the Hunter

The Boss said to Crooked Mick one day, 'Mick, there's a wild bull, an old man 'roo and a dingo playing havoc with the fences and what bit o' feed there is. You're on a fiver if you can clean them up for me.'

'Right-o,' said Mick. 'I'll start in the morning.'

Mick had no ammunition for his rifle so he went round to the station store and collected a box of fifty rounds. 'Be as economical as you can with that ammo,' the Boss urged him. 'We're having a lean season.'

Mick set out on his job early the following morning. He was back by five o'clock in the afternoon. He handed the manager the box of cartridges, remarking casually, 'There you are. Fixed the three of 'em.'

The Boss noticed that only one cartridge had been used from the box. 'Mick,' he said, 'you've only had one shot. You don't mean to tell me you got the bull, the 'roo and the dingo all with one bullet!'

'Too right I did,' Mick declared emphatically. 'All three of 'em!'

'Hell! You must've had a hard job shooting them with one flaming bullet!'

'No,' said Mick, 'shooting 'em wasn't very hard. But getting 'em into line was.'

It was shortly after this episode that a most unfortunate accident befell Crooked Mick.

He was out riding on a fencing job one day when he saw some ducks among the reeds that skirted the Speewah River banks at that point. He had only an old muzzle-loader with him on this occasion.

Mick fired at the birds. The recoil of the old weapon caused him to fall backwards into the river; and he had no sooner touched the water than he was swallowed by a giant cod that was nosing along the bank.

Mick plunged headlong into the darkness. Scrambling to his feet, he presently saw a dim light ahead; and on walking some distance he came upon two swagmen seated at an improvised table, playing cards by the light of a hurricane lamp. Mick nodded to them as they looked up; but they were not the talkative kind of bushmen. One said 'G'day,' and the other mumbled, 'Weather's a bit on the warm side,' and then they resumed their game.

How long Mick might have stayed inside the cod is, to say the least, problematical; but by good fortune some of the Speewah Station hands, out for a day's fishing about two weeks after Crooked Mick's disappearance, hooked the cod with an anchor from one of the discarded paddle-wheeler boats that used to ply up and down the Speewah River in former times. The anchor was sharpened at the points and baited with a bullock, and the men had attached it to a length of twenty-ply steel cable which in turn was fastened to a solid old redgum, 87 feet in diameter.

When the cod was hooked it put up such a fight that, according to the old hands, it straightened out a bend in the river. Be that as it may, it certainly uprooted the old redgum; and I'm told that you can still see the crater where it used to stand. The tree, falling into the water, stunned the cod. In this condition it was hauled out of the river by three teams of bullocks. It never regained consciousness.

Ten days later, the Speewah cooks and their slushies began to cut the flesh from this leviathan to make into fish cutlets. One of the hands suddenly stopped and said, 'I hear a sound like tappin' comin' from the inside!' The men stopped work to listen. And all agreed that someone in the interior of the cod was sending out a message in morse code. When deciphered, it said: 'S.O.S. Oxygen getting low. Crooked Mick.'

Rescue teams went to work; and their surprise was great when they lifted off a particularly large scale and out walked not only Crooked Mick but the two swagmen, complete with billies and pups.

When the Boss heard about it he growled, 'I'll have to sack Mick for this. He had no right to be in there. I didn't give him permission.'

Cougar Tamer

Yup, we usta have quite a bit of trouble with cougars and we wuz pretty keerful to have a gun with us when we ambled out. One time though, I plumb forgot my gun and I had a narrow squeak with one of them-there varmints. 'Twas over to that place I usta have in the valley. I goes out after supper to bring the cows home and I was right dog-eared busy when I happened to look up. There was a cougar comun down the hill after me, and me without a gun. I had to think right smart about it. When the varmint got up to me with wide open mouth I just reached in and grabbed his tail and turned him wrong side out quickern a flash. Of course, he was headed in the wrong direction then, and so doggone surprised that he went lickety-split right back up the hill and out of sight.

A Snake Yarn

'You talk of snakes,' said Jack the Rat,
'But blow me, one hot summer,
I seen a thing that knocked me flat —
Fourteen foot long, or more than that.
It was a regular hummer!
Lay right along a sort of bog,
Just like a log!

'The ugly thing was lyin' there
And not a sign o' movin',
Give any man a nasty scare;
Seen nothing like it anywhere
Since I first started drovin'.
And yet it didn't scare my dog.
Looked like a log!

'I had to cross the bog, you see,
And bluey I was humpin';
But wonderin' what that thing could be
A-laying there in front o' me
I didn't feel like jumpin'.
Yet, though I shivered like a frog,
It *seemed* a log.

'I takes a leap and lands right on
The back of that there whopper!'
He stopped. We waited. Then Big Mac
Remarked, 'Well, then, what happened, Jack?'
'Not much,' said Jack, and drained his grog.
'It was a log!'

XII

Fearsome Critters   128
The Snakebit Hoehandle   133
Cockatoos on the Speewah   133
Fur Trout   134
The Big Wolf   135
Mosquitoes in Australia   136
. . . And America   137
The Wonderful Ointment   138

Fearsome Critters

The Oozlum Bird, a native of Australia, is to be found mainly, as might be expected, on the Speewah. When startled it makes its escape by rising from the ground, where it normally roosts, and flying in ever-decreasing circles until, with a low moan, it disappears inside itself. It is closely related to the American goofus and, like the goofus, has developed the habit of flying backwards. In the oozlum's case, however, it does so not in order to see where it has been but simply to keep the dust of the Speewah out of its eyes.

The Sliver Cat is a large cat with tassled ears and fiery red eyes. It has a very long tail ending in a hard, ball-shaped knob bare on the bottom but with sharp spikes on the top. When hunting, the cat sits on the branch of a tree and clobbers anything passing below on the head with the bare side, picking it up afterwards with the spikes. Not an easy animal to catch.

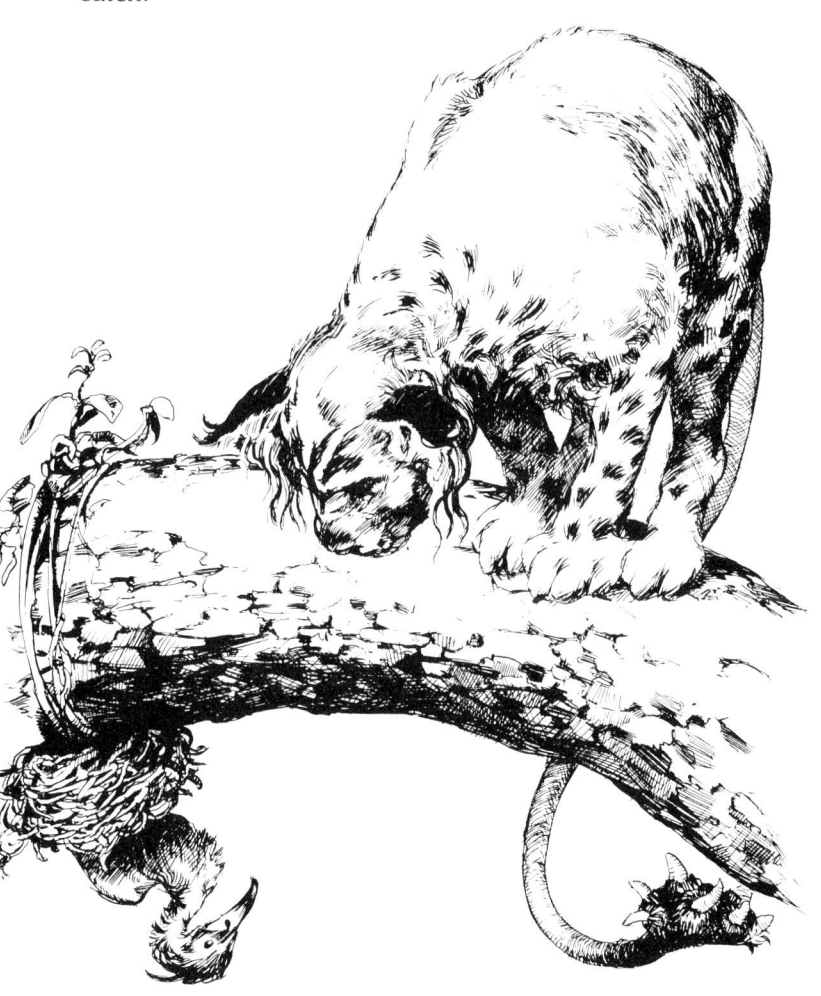

The Goofus Bird, which may now be extinct, seems to have lived mainly near Paul Bunyan's logging camp on the Big Onion River. It was quite different from most other birds in that it built its nest upside down, laid its eggs blunt end first and flew backwards instead of forwards because, as an old lumberjack explained, 'that bird doesn't give a darn where it's going, it only wants to know where it's been'.

The Hoop Snake is sometimes called the *Horn Snake* because its stinger is a spike four or five inches long near the end of its tail. When aroused, and even sometimes when it isn't, it attacks by taking the end of its tail in its mouth to make a hoop and rolling 'like the wind' towards its victim and sticking him with its spike. Its poison is deadly. It has been known to kill a man simply by spiking the stick he was using to fend it off with. One hoop snake chased some children up an apple tree then spiked the tree trunk and waited. When the children became hungry and ate the apples they fell out of the tree, overcome by the poison. In another incident a hoop snake spiked a man's wooden leg, which swelled up so much that he chopped it up and kept himself in firewood for the winter. The only sure way of escaping an attacking hoop snake is to dodge to one side then jump through the hoop as it goes past. If you keep doing this you will confuse the snake so that it will become disheartened and give up. Although a native of the United States, the hoop snake is also found on the Speewah in Australia. No one knows how it got there.

The Sidehill Dodger (sometimes called the *Gwinter*) is something like a cross between a buffalo and a mountain goat. It lives in the mountains and is unusual in that its downhill legs are longer than the uphill ones. This makes it easier for the dodger to move on the steep mountain slopes but it can only go in one direction. It was once thought that there were two sorts of dodger — the left-handed, or clockwise, and the right-handed, or anti-clockwise — but it is now known that they are the same animal. When a left-handed dodger, say, reaches the top of its mountain it simply turns itself inside out, becoming right-handed in the process, and goes back down the other way. Sidehill dodgers are very fierce, but not difficult to catch. All you have to do is take two steps downhill when one charges at you. It can't run the other way, so either it goes all the way round the mountain to come at you again, so wearing itself out, or it forgets, tries to turn round, and falls over. But there's not a lot you can do with a dodger when you've caught it.

The Hugag, another inhabitant of the United States, is a huge animal but fortunately not carnivorous. It can't lie down because it doesn't have any joints in its legs so it rests and sleeps by leaning against anything handy — sheds, houses, fences, but mainly trees — making them lean to one side. Hunting them is a highly skilled job depending for success on months of unobtrusive observation to discover their favourite resting trees. Such a tree is then partially cut through so that when a hugag returns to rest it pushes the tree over, falling down with it. Once down it cannot get up again.

The Hidebehind is very dangerous, stalking its prey through the North American lumber camps. It gets its name partly from the fact that it is always hiding behind something — usually a tree — but partly also because it's always behind you whichever way you turn. A deadly creature but no one knows what it looks like because no one has ever seen it.

The Snakebit Hoehandle

Copperhead made for me one day when I was hoein' my corn. Happened I saw him in time and I lit into him with the hoe. He thrashed around; bit the hoehandle a couple of times, but I fin'lly killed him. Hung him on the fence.

Went on back to work, and directly my hoehandle felt thicker'n common. I looked it over good and it was swellin'. The poison from that snakebite was workin' all through it. After I tried it a few more licks it popped the shank and the hoe-head fell off. So I threw that handle over by the fence: went and fixed me another'n. Got my corn hoed out about dark.

Week or two after that I was lookin' over my cornfield and I noticed a log in the fencerow. Examined it right close and blame if it wasn't that hoehandle! Hit was swelled up big enough for lumber. So I took it and had it sawed. Had enough boards to build me a new chicken house. Then I painted it and, don't you know! — the turpentine in the paint took out all that swellin', and the next mornin' my chicken house had shrunk to the size of a shoe box. — Good thing I hadn't put my chickens in it!

Cockatoos on the Speewah

'Y'oughter see the cockatoos at Speewah,' said the old man. 'Cripes! They wus thick. There was so many of them that if they flew over when it was raining, not a drop touched the ground for a mile around.

'When they landed to feed, one always kept guard so you couldn't get near enough to shoot them.

'They always landed on a big, dry, red-gum when you frightened them, so the boss covered that red-gum from top to bottom with bird lime.

'Next day when the cockatoos landed on it he ran down with his gun. Just as he was going to fire they took off and tore that tree up by the roots. The last the boss saw of that tree it was about a mile up, making south.'

Fur Trout

You've probably heard that in parts of New England it gets so cold in winter that the trout grow fur coats. Well, I don't believe a word of it. Those people up in Maine are always complaining about something. They even complain that it sometimes freezes so suddenly that the ice is still warm (and if you can grumble about warm ice there's nothing will satisfy you).

But down in Arkansas there really are fur trout. A yankee pedlar moved in years ago and set up business on a branch of the Arkansas River. He was one of these quack doctors who used to travel around with bottles of medicine guaranteed to cure everything from in-growing toenails to baldness. When he died he hadn't made his fortune and there were just as many sufferers in the area as there had been before he came.

It was only after he died that fisherman began, occasionally, to pull fur trout out of the Arkansas River: fighting fish with shaggy fur from gill to tail and, in some specimens, beard and moustache as well. They never did catch many, though, until they cottoned on to the link between the pedlar and the fish. You see, when he died all his bottles were emptied into the river. So if you want to be sure of a good catch you go down to the river on a Saturday afternoon, put on a white coat, stick a red and white pole in the bank, wave a pair of scissors in the air and yell 'Next!'

The Big Wolf

Yes, I'n tell you about wolves. My partner and me, we went up in the Sawtooths and got two elk and was headun home when we looked around and seen eleven wolves after us. We cut a elk loose and they et that. In another mile we give them the other elk and they et that. Then we left our horses and run for it, and they came up and et the horses. I said to my partner that I would rest and shoot a wolf and then run while he was restun and then he could shoot one. So we did. I shot one and the wolves pounced on it while I was runnin; and then my partner, he shot one. Well, we kept that up till we had shot ten of them. Then my partner yelled, 'God a-mighty, Jim, look!' I looked behind me and there right on our tails was the biggest wolf anybody ever laid eyes on. He was as big as a house. And then I remembered he'd have to be that big, seeing as how he'd et two elk, two horses, and ten wolves.

Mosquitoes in Australia

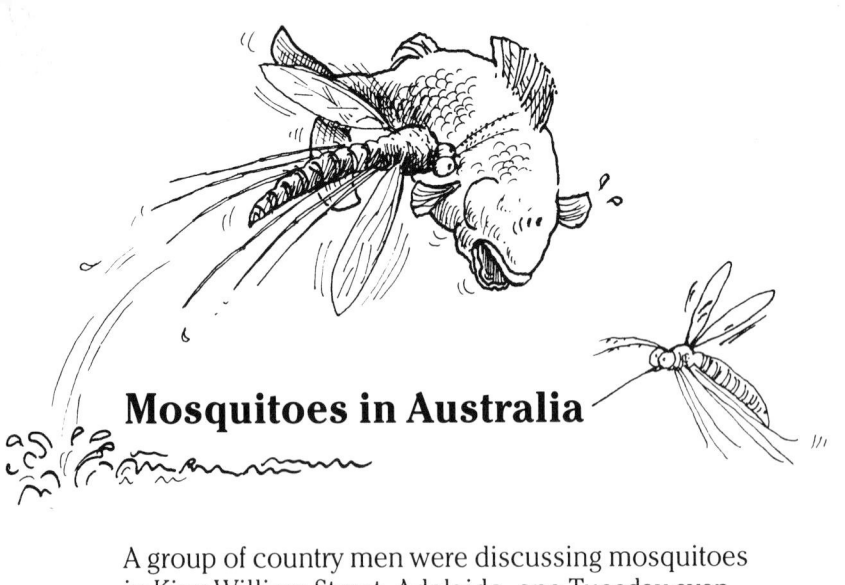

A group of country men were discussing mosquitoes in King William Street, Adelaide, one Tuesday evening. 'Yas,' said a burly northerner, 'I ain't seen no skeeters to equal them we 'ave up above. Now, look 'ere; there's an old stagnant dam on my farm, and at night yer ken hear the skeeters splashin' about in the water like birds. In fact, a new 'and I got last week shot a couple of 'em just afore dark one night, thinkin' they was ducks.'

'That's nothing,' observed a thin, sunburnt little man with a squint; 'over round Lake Wangary, on the west coast, yer can 'ear 'em goin' to roost on the fences at night. They make the wires twang like banjos; straight iron.'

'Wal,' said a lanky individual, whose chief adornments were bell-bottomed trousers and an enormous tent of a hat, 'yer wanter go along the Murray for them insects. On that strip of wetness yer git 'em big and good. 'Tain't nothin' jest 'afore sundown to see a moskeeto dive into the Murray and come up and fly away with a 20-lb. cod. They never miss 'em!'

The last man now chipped in — a stout, dark person in a cork fly net. 'sorry to 'ear yer've got sech small miskeeters in your districts — very sorry, indeed. Now, if yer want real sizeable miskeeters jest go across to Yorke Peninsula. They seen to fatten up wonderful on Cornishmen. I was campin' over there in a tent last week, and about midnight I was woke up by a hummin' noise, like a motor car doin' a record, and next minute a small miskeeter settled on me chest. "'Ere," I yelled to me mate, "give us a 'and; there's a miskeeter dropped on me." "Well, knock 'im off," 'e sez. "'Ow ken I," sez I, "when 'e's got both me 'ands pinned down!" '

... And America

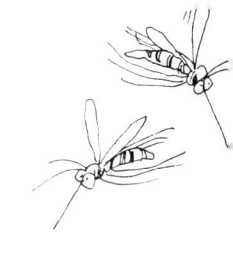

I was sleeping one night when a loud noise at my door woke me up. It was somebody knocking and telling me to let them in because they wanted something to eat. Well, I thought that it was some guys from down the hall. I was so sleepy I just hollered out there, 'Say, man, get your hungry self away from that door!' But I saw they didn't go. Instead, they started pushing on the door and talking loud. The voices I heard out there *did* sound kind of strange, but that didn't bother me much.

Finally they broke on in. It was two great *big* mosquitoes. I had always heard that if you carry a lighted torch, mosquitoes won't bite you. When I saw those two cats walk over there and stand over my bed, I decided to find out if there was any truth to what I had heard. I said to them, 'Say man, is it true that if I light a torch and carry it, you can't bite me?'

'That depends on how fast you carry that torch, Jack.' That's what they told me.

Well, they drug me off the bed. I heard one of them say real low, 'Man do you think we should eat this cat here, or take him down to the field and eat him?'

'I think you must be crazy! You know as well as I do that if we take him to the field, that them *big* mosquitoes will take him away from us!'

We can't keep cows any more. After the last one disappeared we saw half-a-dozen mosquitoes sitting on a log using the horns for tooth-picks.

The Wonderful Ointment

'Yes, sir,' began old Uncle Noah, 'them surgeons over in France did some right clever patchin' up of our soljers, but I'll bet if old Doc Goodfellow hadda gone over he'd beat the hull lot. Did I ever tell you about his wonderful growin' ointment? No? The time he made his big hit at the Territorial Fair? Well, you see, some boys were puttin' a tame coyote into a pen when his tail caught in the door and was cut plumb off at the roots.

'I'll tell you them boys felt bad, and the coyote wasn't very cheerful himself. They sent for old Doc Goodfellow, of course, and the Doc rubbed some of his growing ointment on the stub, and blame my cats if a new tail didn't grow right out while they was watchin' it.

'Then them boys had a fine idea, and rubbed some of the stuff on the cut place on the tail, and sure as I'm a truthful man, another coyote grew out of the tail, only' — here Uncle Noah spat reminiscently — 'he was a wild coyote and they had to kill him.'

> Colorado is a bigger state than Texas. God laid Texas out flat, but to get Colorado into the State lines He had to crumple it all up. That's why the mountains are there.

XIII

Skunk Oil's Punkin   139
Paul Bunyan's Cornstalk   143
The Crookest Raffle ever run in Australia   147
Uncle Jasper and the Watermelon Bet   152

Skunk Oil's Punkin

One of the first men I met after I had settled in Chase County, in the southwest corner of Nebraska, in the 1880s was an old fellow who had a claim on the Stinking Water River. He was a character who did a little bit of everything from trapping and hunting to farming, but what he excelled in the most was lying. He could think up more lies in less time than anyone I have ever known. And I have heard some pretty good deviations from the truth in my day. But this man was the champion.

I don't recall his real name, nor would it matter if I did because to everyone in the community he was known as 'Skunk Oil.' He had been given this name because of his constant claims that a skunk's oil had the power to cure all diseases. Besides, Skunk Oil carried a bad odour with him — caused, I think, by his lack of interest in bathing. Then, too, he was constantly sweating, even in the coldest weather. It wasn't a pretty sight — or smell! But it was, so to speak, Skunk Oil's trade mark, and as that you had to accept it.

One day when I was out looking over the land in preparation for spring ploughing, I saw Skunk Oil ambling along an old buffalo trail which led past my place. I had only met him once before, and I knew I was in for another lie, since a new comer to the county was always legitimate prey for Skunk Oil.

But Skunk Oil, after our preliminary greetings were over, fooled around a while talking about this and that before he got around to the whopper that I knew he was itching to tell. You see, I had met up with him once before on the first day of my arrival in the county, so I knew what he was leading up to. He finally got started by asking what I thought of the country and its possibilities. I answered by telling him I didn't think anyone could raise much but grass and, with luck, maybe a little hell.

'Man, you're plumb wrong there,' was his reply. 'Ever hear about them punkins I raised over by the river? Well, you ought to have seen them.'

I saw he was starting to warm up to his subject, so I looked doubtful and said I didn't think they'd grow over there. He didn't reply for a moment or so because he was busy biting off a chew of navy plug that apparently was as tough as leather. Then, after he had succeeded in chewing off a big piece, he slowly replied, 'I didn't think they would grow there myself, so I didn't attempt planting any punkin seeds. But one day when I was dropping some corn seed along the river, seven or eight punkin seeds showed up in the poke of corn , so I naturally planted those seeds with the corn and forgot about them. The corn grew up and by the middle of the summer was better'n shoulder high. But I didn't go over to the field for a long time. I believed in letting good enough be, so let the corn take care of itself. Besides, I was having a great deal of pig trouble at this time.'

'How was that?' I asked.

'Well, I had an old sow who had a litter of eleven little pigs that I turned loose to forage for themselves. It saved me the trouble of feeding them. For a while they stayed near the house, but one day they didn't show up and it was the beginning of no end of trouble. I spent several weeks looking for them, but couldn't find so much as a trace of their whereabouts. Along in September I went to my corn patch by the river, and what I saw nearly made me doubt my sanity.'

'Why, what had happened?'

'The eight punkin seeds that had been mixed in with the seed corn I had planted had started growing in a big way, like the bean in 'Jack and the Beanstalk,' only for me they followed the ground. One punkin vine was especially big. It was at least eight foot thick and took off across the river like a big green snake, disappearing in a thicket on the opposite side of the river bank. This vine was so enormous that its top was above my head. I followed it to the bank, where I crawled up on it and walked across the river. It made a natural bridge which was strong enough to hold a team of oxen.

'Well, believe it or not, I followed this vine for seven miles into the open prairie, where, at its end, I found a tremendous punkin which must have been at least thirty feet high. It was a beautiful reddish-yellow, ripening in the fall air. From a distance, with the sun shining on it, it looked very much like a harvest moon. I had never seen anything like it before and probably never will again.

'As I was walking around it, looking it over, I heard a grunting, squealing sound come from its insides. It was a peculiar, unearthly noise, which had me scared stiff for a few minutes until I happened to think of my missing pigs. It was them I heard. They were in the punkin, although I couldn't figure out how they had gotten there.

'So I hurried back to the house for a saw and axe, which I took back to the punkin. After two hours of sawing and cutting I managed to make a hole in the side. It was hard work, because the punkin's sides were hard as plate iron. After I had finished making a good-sized hole, I crawled inside where, sure's you're born, were those pigs. They had growed so it was difficult to recognize them. Must have weighed two hundred pounds apiece, while the sow probably tipped the scales at half a ton.

'Now that I found my pigs, I was sure hankering to find out how they had gotten into the punkin. Nor did it take me long to get at the secret. The old sow had taken her litter to the corn patch, where, when rooting around, she'd dug a hole into the side of the vine and had gone inside, followed by her pigs. Here they stayed, feeding on the vine and growing along with it. In time it carried them across the river to the big punkin itself. This they made their headquarters. But there were many tracks in the vine itself, so they probably travelled back and forth a great deal.

'The punkin was too big to move, so I left the pigs there all winter and they used it for a snug, cozy hog house. I walked over once a week to see how they were getting along. When the weather was nice, I walked over on the top of the vine, but when it was cold, I lighted a miner's lamp, which I had purchased from an old pedlar, and used the inside of the vine. It made a fine tunnel.

'When spring came, I hitched the team to my wagon and crossed the river on the vine — it was a perfect road — with the idea of loading one of the punkin seeds for another crop. I took Hank Billings, who lived up the river a ways, along to help me load the seed.

'Unfortunately we didn't have a rope and pulley so were forced to raise the punkin seed with our hands. The seed slipped during the process and caught Hank under it, breaking his leg. Naturally this accident made him good and mad since it meant he would be laid up for the greater part of the summer.

'So I was not surprised the next day when a committee of settlers called at my house and ordered me not to plant any more punkins. They said they were skeered of the punkin taking over the whole county if any more grew like the last one did, and there wasn't any sense in taking any unnecessary risks.

'I tried to answer their arguments by telling them what fine roads and bridges the vines would make and of the punkin houses and barns that could be made from the heads, but they wouldn't listen to me and burned all my seeds. So I calculate the only punkins we will have from now on will be the ordinary garden variety, which isn't good for anything except pies.'

> **Trees in California are so big they're hinged to let the sun go by.**

1. PAUL BUNYAN WAS THE GREAT HERO OF THE NORTH AMERICAN LUMBER CAMPS. NOTHING PAUL EVER DID WAS SMALL!

2. HE COULD TOP AND FELL TEN TREES WHILE THE NEXT MAN WAS TIGHTENING HIS BELT!!

3. THE CORNSEED HE PLANTED ONE YEAR WAS GOING TO BECOME THE **FASTEST**-GROWING CORNSTALK EVER!

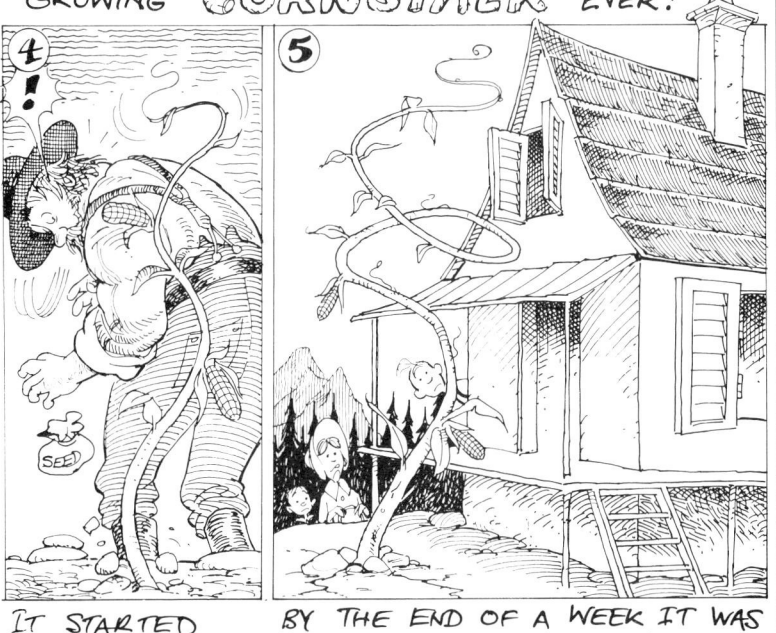

4. IT STARTED TO GROW IMMEDIATELY!

5. BY THE END OF A WEEK IT WAS AS TALL AS THE HOUSE! FOLKS CAME TO WATCH IT GROW!

6
?
SLURP!
THE ROOTS STARTED SUCKING WATER FROM ALL AROUND..
7
EVEN THE GREAT LAKES WERE SUCKED DRY
10
... AND DEMANDED THAT PAUL CHOP HIS CORNSTALK DOWN!
11
TROUBLE WAS . .
14
PAUL FIGURED THE ONLY WAY WAS TO CLIMB UP AND CHOP OFF THE TOP.
15
AFTER TWO DAYS, FOLKS BEGAN TO CALL . . . .

8
!
9
MUTTER
MUTTER
THINGS GOT SO BAD.....
THAT THE FOLKS GOT MAD.....
12
13
!
IT WAS GROWING SO FAST... THAT EACH NOTCH...
WAS OUT OF REACH BEFORE HE COULD DEEPEN IT!
PAUL?
16
ZZZZZ
PAUL?
AFTER FOUR DAYS, THERE WAS STILL NO SIGN!

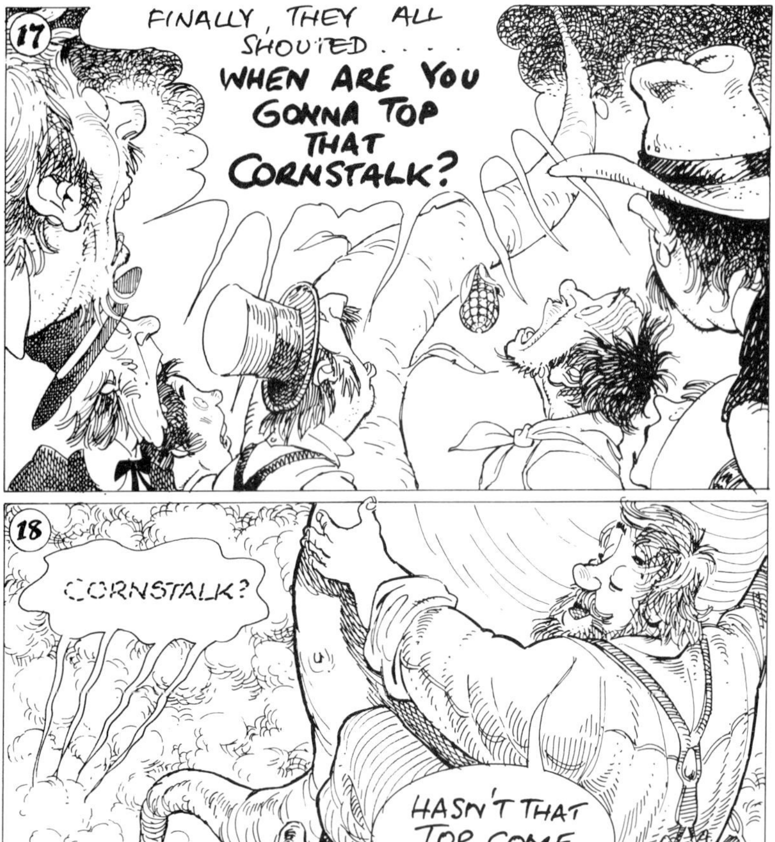

SO THINGS GOT BACK TO NORMAL . . . .
BUT IT WAS A NARROW ESCAPE!

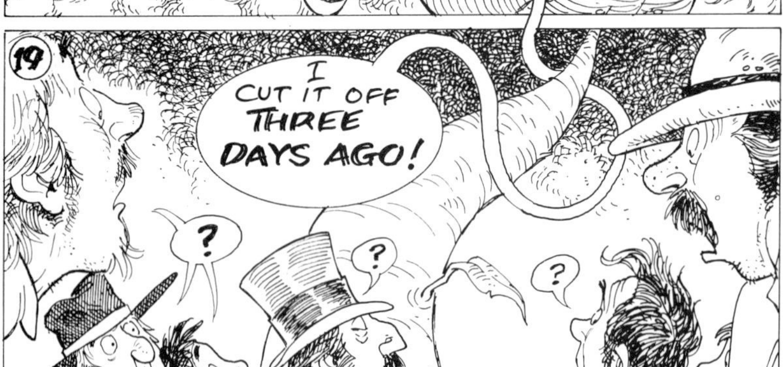

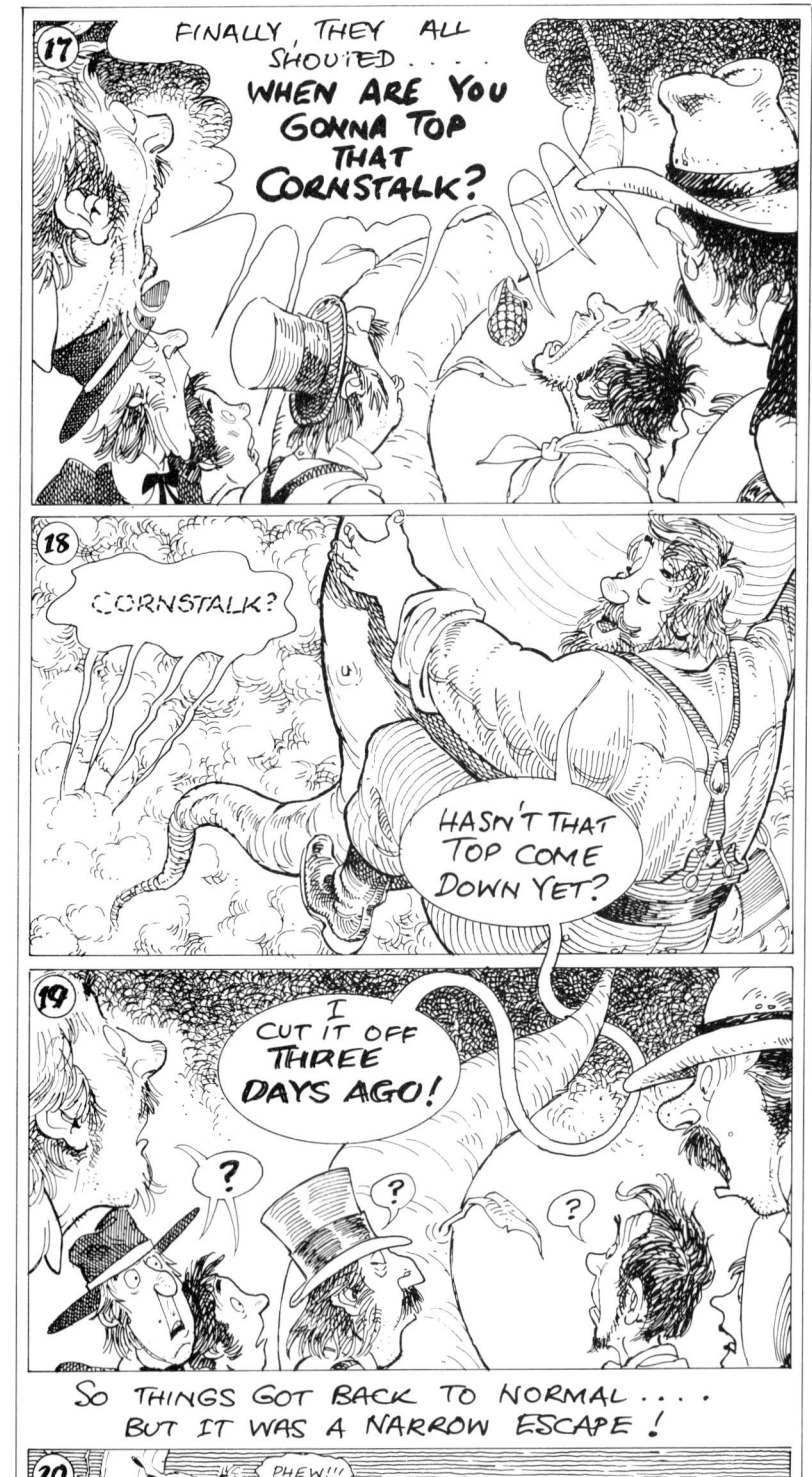

The Crookest Raffle ever run in Australia

'Did I ever tell yer about the crookest raffle every run in Australia?'

'No, but you told me about the only fair dinkum one.'

'That's a different raffle altogether. That's the one I ran at Woolloomooloo during the Depression.'

'You'd better have a drink.'

'Don't mind if I do. Well, this here raffle I'm talking about was for a pumpkin and it was run in a place called Benson's Valley. It was run by a fella called Trigger MacIntosh. Don't know how he go that nickname but I know he had thirteen kids. Little fella. Bald as a billiard ball.'

'But people wouldn't buy a ticket in a raffle for a pumpkin surely.'

'Australians will buy a raffle ticket in anything. They got into the habit during the Depression. Buying raffle tickets is like going to church or drinking beer, once you get into the habit. . . . Anyway, this was a special pumpkin. The biggest pumpkin ever grown in the history of the world. It was so big it took six men six hours to dig it out of the ground.'

'But pumpkins don't grow under the ground.'

'I know that, but this one was so heavy it sunk into the ground till you couldn't see it.'

'You don't say.'

'If you don't believe me you can ask Trigger MacIntosh. He grew that pumpkin, brother. I'm telling you: it took six men six hours to dig . . .'

'You told me that.'

'Yeh, but it took the same six men another six hours to roll it up six planks on to a six-ton truck to take it to the pub to be raffled. But my father always said: 'Never get ahead of your story.' So first I must tell you how they came to grow this here pumpkin.'

'They? But you said this bloke grew it himself. What did you say his name was?'

'Trigger MacIntosh. Matter of fact, Trigger didn't grow this pumpkin at all. He owned it in partnership with another fella — name of Greenfingers Stratton. Old Greenfingers could grow a crop of show orchids on a concrete footpath, so my father reckoned. Well, one day Trigger said to Greenfingers: 'I know where I can borrow a block of land and start a market garden.' Fancy mentioning a block of land to old Greenfingers — always saying 'If only I had a block of land, I'd grow somethin', I can tell yer.' Funny how people never fulfil their ambitions. I knew a violinist once who wanted to be a League footballer. . . .'

'You've told me about him. Have another drink and get on with your story. . . .'

'Well, it turned out that Trigger had talked an old man with more money than sense into lending him some land on the river bank. Very rich soil from the floods that happened every few years. Well, they decided to grow pumpkins, for some reason, and Greenfingers went to work. Pretty soon pumpkin vines began to crawl all over the property, across the creek, over some paddocks of lucerne, up the side of the old man's house and down the road towards the pub. Well, anyhow, Trigger and Greenfingers waited for the pumpkins to grow but nothing happened until one day one solitary pumpkin began to grow right in the middle of the paddock. It grew so fast you could see it bulging. It became so heavy it began to sink into the ground. And eventually it took six men . . .'

'Yes, I know, six men six hours to dig it out.'

'That's right, and the same six men another six hours to roll it up six planks on to a six-ton truck to take it down to the pub.'

'All right. Why didn't they sell the pumpkin or enter it in the Royal Show?'

'What? Made a lot of money raffling it six times — that's why! Anyway down to the pub they went with it. A'course, it wouldn't fit in the pub door, needless to say, so they left it on the truck outside. And Trigger put a sign on it: *The Biggest Pumpkin ever Grew —*

6d. A Ticket. Bought six raffle books at the newsagent's with a hundred tickets in each. . . .'

'Did they sell all the tickets?'

'For sure! In the pub. The pumpkin being so big and people being in the habit of buying raffle tickets, like I told you. There was a crowd around that pumpkin all day outside the Royal Hotel and during the afternoon six blokes got on top of it and sat in the sun drinking beer. Just before closing time, the raffle was drawn.'

'Who won it?'

'Old Greenfingers himself, naturally, seeing Trigger drew the ticket out of the kerosene tin he had for the purpose and seeing it was the crookest raffle ever run in Australia, as I said before. Eventually they raffled the pumpkin six times. If you don't believe me you can ask Trigger MacIntosh. . . .'

'And I suppose this bloke Greenfingers won it every time?'

'No, he only won it five times.'

'Well, who won it the other time?'

'Well, I'll tell you. Greenfingers Stratton won the first raffle on account of Trigger MacIntosh had a ticket with a secret mark on it. Anyway, the next Saturday they brought the pumpkin back to the pub again.'

'Be a bit awkward wouldn't it? Raffling the biggest pumpkin ever grew more than once.'

'Matterafact, they changed the sign to read '*The Second Biggest Pumpkin ever Grew*', and sold six hundred tickets again and old Greenfingers won it. The next Saturday, they raffled the third biggest pumpkin ever grew, and so on, until they arrived at the pub one Saturday morning with the sixth biggest pumpkin ever grew.'

'You don't mean to say . . .'

'If you don't believe me, you can ask Greenfingers. . . .'

'I believe you but thousands wouldn't. Go on; who won it the sixth time?'

'Needless to say, that there pumpkin was becoming a bit the worse for wear what with rolling it on and off the truck, and people climbing up on to it to drink their beer. It was bruised and battered, so my father reckoned. Trigger MacIntosh said afterwards it seemed to have a face and used to snarl at him when he walked past it. Now, for some reason certain people, wowsers and the like, started to say the raffles weren't fair dinkum.'

'You don't tell me.'

'It's a fact. There's no pleasing some people. Anyhow, my father reckoned that Danny O'Connell, the publican, said to Trigger: 'Listen, that there sixth biggest pumpkin that ever grew. I seem to have seen it somewhere before.' 'A simple case of mistaken identity,' Trigger told him. He was as quick as a flash, was Trigger. Did I ever tell about the time Trigger came in late at a concert in Melbourne?'

'No, I don't think you did. Just tell me about the sixth raffle. I'll settle for that.'

'Well, O'Connell didn't like raffles being run in his pub on account his customers had only so much money to spend and he liked them to spend it on his beer. So he says to Trigger: 'Some of my customers are complaining. They say Greenfingers Stratton won your raffle five weeks in a row.'

'Trigger had a good answer as usual. He said: 'Old Greenfingers was always lucky.' 'Yeh,' O'Connell replied, 'and he's working with a very lucky partner too, if you ask me.' 'No one asked you, as it turns out,' Trigger told him, 'but at least we haven't watered that pumpkin and put a collar on it like you do with your beer.' You couldn't beat old Trigger in an argument and that's for sure. Anyway, in spite of some bad publicity, they sold six books of tickets. Then, just when Trigger was going to draw Greenfingers' ticket out of the tin, Danny O'Connell said: 'Just a minute, I'll draw the raffle this week.' Well you can imagine how Trigger felt. He loses all his capital if someone wins that pumpkin off him. So he says: 'I don't like no aspersions being cast on my character, but you can draw it, if you insist.' And he was thinking fast. 'You can draw it at five to six.'

'What difference did it make when he drew it?'

'A lot of difference. Trigger calls Greenfingers aside. "Here," he says, "here's six more raffle books. Go and lock yourself in the dunny and fill out every ticket in my name."'

'So old Trigger won the sixth raffle himself?'

'As a matter of fact, a bloke named Sniffy Connors won the raffle with the only ticket he ever bought in his life. Greenfingers got writer's cramp filling in six hundred butts. Trigger had half of the tickets but, as luck would have it, O'Connell drew out the one Sniffy Connors bought.'

'And what did Sniffy do with the pumpkin? Eat it?'

'Sniffy was living in a tent at the time, so he blew a hole in the side of the pumpkin with a stick of gelignite and made a house out of it. Lived in it for six years with his wife and six kids. . . . I could take you to the spot and show you the house except he got burnt out in the bushfires in 1936.'

'You win. Have another beer.'

'Not me. I'm busy today. Running a raffle. The biggest turkey ever bred in Australia. Two bob a time. How many tickets do you want?'

> Out where I come from it only takes four eggs to make a dozen.

Uncle Jasper and the Watermelon Bet

Quite a few watermelons are raised in the state of South Carolina, but one of the counties where they thrive best in Barnwell County. During the season, a large number of people in the small towns make a business of selling watermelons. Most of them usually buy a large melon on Saturday and carry it home to use as part of their Sunday dinner. The watermelon business is so prosperous that many of the vendors buy an entire wagonload at a time.

One of the best watermelon pedlars in the county was a white man at Allendale by the name of Dillon. Most of the blacks in Allendale bought their melons from him because he had special ways of attracting their attention and getting them interested in buying.

There was only one time that he made a mistake in his advertising methods, and that was one Saturday when he picked up a big forty-pound watermelon from his wagon and said, 'I'll give anybody who can eat this whole melon to the rind a ten dollar bill, but under one condition only: if he fails to eat it to the rind he will have to pay me a dollar for the melon.'

No one said anything at first, but finally an old man by the name of Uncle Jasper got up off the box he was sitting on and said, 'Will you gimme ten minutes to decide?'

'Sure,' replied Dillon. So Uncle Jasper left. In exactly ten minutes he came back and announced that he was ready to eat the forty-pound melon. Dillon handed it to him and he ate it to the rind in about four minutes.

Dillon, who was very much surprised that Uncle Jasper was able to eat the large watermelon, and who hated to pay him the ten dollars that he had promised, said, 'Uncle Jasper, I'm gonna pay you the ten dollars all right, but before I pay you I'd like to know why you wanted ten minutes to decide.'

'Well,' replied Uncle Jasper, 'I knowed that I had one at home that weighed forty pounds, so I went home an' et that un, an' I knowed ef I et that un, I c'd eat this un, too.'

'The wind Ah seen on the East Coast blowed a crooked road straight and blowed a well up out the ground and blowed and blowed until it scattered the days of the week so bad till Sunday didn't come till late Tuesday evenin'.'

Notes and acknowledgements

I wish to thank the following for their permission to reprint copyright material. For this collection I have sometimes altered the original texts. In the notes that follow I have used the terms *adapted* to indicate minor editorial changes and *retold* for a more substantial rewriting. Where I have simply stated the source I have made no changes.

1
'The Wheelbarrow Boy' by Richard Parker from *Magazine of Fantasy and Science Fiction* © 1953 Richard Parker. Reprinted by permission of Curtis Brown Ltd., London.
'The Lesson' by Roger McGough from *in the glassroom* (Cape 1976). Reprinted by permission of A D Peters and Company Ltd.
'The Tortoise' by Robert Scott © 1987
'The Bite' by Robert Scott © 1987
'The Gingerbread House Caper' by Will Stanton from *Once Upon A Time is Enough*, J B Lippincott 1979. Reprinted by permission of the author. Slightly adapted.
'The Lion and Albert' by Marriott Edgar. From Michael Marshall (ed.): *The Stanley Holloway Monologues*, Elm Tree Books 1979. Copyright 1932 Francis Day and Hunter Ltd. Reprinted by permission of EMI Music Publishing Ltd., London.

2
'Wait Till Martin Comes' from Basil Davenport (ed): *Tales to be Told in the Dark*, Faber & Faber 1953. Slightly adapted. A Black American version of this tale, 'Wait Till Emmett Comes', is in Tristram P Coffin & Hennig Cohen (eds): *Folklore in America*, Doubleday & Co., Inc. 1966.
'The Yellow Ribbon' by Robert Scott © 1987
'The Four Hunchbacks' from Harold Courlander: *The Drum and the Hoe.* Copyright 1960 Harold Courlander. By permission of the University of California Press.
'A Family Pet' from the Federal Writers' project: *Idaho Lore* The Caxton Printers, Ltd © 1939 George H Curtis. Reprinted from B A Botkin: *A Treasury of American Folklore*, Crown Publishers 1944.
'The Helpful Undertaker' by Robert Scott © 1985

3
'Cap'n Santos' Leg' from Jeremiah Digges: *Cape Cod Pilot*, Federal Writers' Project. Viking Press © 1937 Poor Richard Associates. Reprinted from B A Botkin: *A Treasury of American Folklore*, Crown Publishers 1944.
'Raymond and Nellie' from H H Lee and D Roberson (eds): *Lore of Our Land*, Harper & Row 1963. Reprinted by permission of the editors. Slightly adapted. The story is based on one of the most widely distributed urban legends. See Jan Harold Brunvand: *The Vanishing Hitchhiker*, Pan Books Ltd 1983, for versions of this and other legends.

'The Twins' by Henry Sambroke Leigh
'Framed in a First-storey Winder' Anon.
'The Telltale Seaweed' by Alexander Woollcott from *While Rome Burns* Viking Press 1934, where it is called 'Full Fathom Five'. Copyright 1934 by Alexander Woollcott, renewed © 1962 by Joseph P. Hennesey. Reprinted by permission of Viking Penguin Inc. The adapted version I have used is that printed in *The 'Life' Treasury of American Folklore*, Time Publications 1961.

4

'The Motor Mechanic' by Carl MacDougall from *A Scent of Water* (Molendinar Press 1975). Adapted. I have included about half of MacDougall's story of Joe MacHinery.
'The Kluge Maker' This 'shaggy dog' was very popular in America in the 1940s. The version I have used is that retold by Alvin Schwartz from the *New York Folklore Quarterly* volume III, number 4, winter 1947. By permission of the New York Folklore Society and the editor of *New York Folklore*.
'The High Divers' by Jack Conroy from manuscripts of the Federal Writers' Project. Reprinted from B A Botkin: *A Treasury of American Folklore* Copyright © 1944, 1972, by B A Botkin. Reprinted by permission of Crown Publishers Inc. Conroy heard the story from a circus clown and strong man.
'The Fish Merchant' from Henry D Spalding: *Encyclopaedia of Black Folklore and Humour*, Jonathan David Publishers 1972. Slightly adapted. Spalding does not give his source but notes that Bert Williams was a celebrated vaudeville (Music Hall) performer at the turn of the century.
'The Yankee Painter' from *Yankee Blade*, 16th December, 1854 (vol. xiv) and reprinted in R M Dorson: *Jonathan Draws the Long Bow*, Harvard University Press/Oxford University Press 1946. Slightly adapted.

5

'Lizzie's Lion' by © Dennis Lee. Taken from Brian Patten (ed): *Gangsters, Ghosts & Dragonflies*, Allen & Unwin 1981. Copyright 1981 by Dennis Lee. Reprinted by permission of the author.
'León and the Lion' The tale was collected by Octavio Romano, *New Mexico Folklore Record* vol. 6, and adapted by Maria Leach for *The Rainbow Book of American Folk Tales and Legends*, World Publishing Co. 1958. Reprinted by permission of Philomel Books. I have reprinted Leach's version.
'The Pet Rattlesnake' from *Idaho Lore*. See the note on 'A Family Pet'.
'The Mare's Egg' — a traditional story from Sussex.
'The Horse' by Robert Scott © 1987. There is a Black American version, called 'The Horse with Strange Compulsions' in Henry D Spalding: *Encyclopaedia of Black American Folklore and Humour*.
'Grant's Tame Trout' Ed Grant's tale was collected by Francis I Maule: *The Tame Trout and other Backwoods Fairy Tales*, Farmington 1941 and reprinted by R M Dorson: *Jonathan Draws the Long Bow*. Reprinted by permission of Harvard University Press. Slightly adapted. There are many versions of this tale, all

with the same sad end. Dal Stivens, in his Australian story 'Sammy, the Sand Mullet' has Sammy learning to herd sheep. Gary Cooper told the story when playing Wild Bill Hickok in the film 'The Plainsman'.
'Blue Cloud's Cat' from E C Beck: *They Knew Paul Bunyan* (1956). Reprinted by permission of The University of Michigan Press. Adapted.
'Pablo Romero Roped a Bear' by J Frank Dobie from *I'll Tell You a Tale*. Copyright 1928, 1930, 1931, 1935, 1936, 1938, 1939, 1941, 1947, 1949, 1950, 1951, 1952, 1955, © 1960 by J Frank Dobie. Reprinted by permission of Little, Brown and Co.

6
'If You Want to Live for Ever' by Sholom Aleichem from his story 'The Town of the Little People' collected in *The Old Country*. Copyright © 1946, 1974, by Crown Publishers Inc. Reprinted by permission of Crown Publishers Inc.
'The Cake' appeared originally in *The Hobo News, A Little Fun to Match the Sorrow*, vol. 2 (May, 1953) No 78, page 8. Copyright 1952 by The Hobo News, Newark, New Jersey. I have taken it from B A Botkin: *A Treasury of American Anecdotes*, Random House 1957
'To Save Time' — a traditional Jewish anecdote.
'The Lobster' by Robert Scott © 1987
'The Patcham Treacle Mines' appears in a letter by Mrs J M Austen to the *West Sussex Gazette* of 12th July 1973. I have taken it from an article by Jacqueline Simpson: 'Multi-purpose Treacle Mines in Sussex and Surrey' in *Lore and Language* vol. 3, no. 6 Part A, January 1982. (CECTAL, University of Sheffield)

7
'The Horse who Played Cricket' collected by Katharine Briggs in 1963 and included in Katharine M Briggs & Ruth L Tongue (eds): *Folktales of England*. Copyright 1965 by The University of Chicago. Reprinted with permission. A literary version is given by Eric Partridge in *The 'Shaggy Dog' Story* (Faber and Faber 1953). He mentions an American tale in which the game is baseball and the horse can't *pitch*.
'The Cow Mechanic' by Robert Scott © 1987
'The Scholarly Mouse' by Dal Stivens from *The Scholarly Mouse and Other Tales*, Angus & Robertson 1957 and 'The Smart Dog' by Dal Stivens from *Selected Stories 1936–1968*. Reprinted by permission of Curtis Brown (Aust.) Pty. Ltd. Sydney.
'John and the Blacksnake' collected by Harold Courlander and printed in his *Treasury of Afro-American Folklore*. Copyright © 1976 by Harold Courlander. Reprinted by permission of Crown Publishers Inc.

8
'The Old Lady' Retold from a version collected by Lowell Thomas: *Tall Stories*, Harvest House, 1945
'Jonah and the Whale' by Gareth Owen from *Salford Road* (Kestrel Books, 1979). Reprinted by permission of the author.
'The Lady and the Cowboy' by John D Higinbotham from *When*

the West was Young, The Ryerson Press. Reprinted by permission of Norman Higinbotham. Adapted.

'Morris' This story was collected by B A Botkin in New York in 1957 and printed in his *A Treasury of American Anecdotes*, Random House 1957. Copyright 1957 by B A Botkin. Reprinted by permission of Curtis Brown Ltd. Slightly adapted. Eric Partridge, in *The 'Shaggy Dog' Story*, has an Irish version of this tale: 'Paddy's visit to Rome'.

'Old Master and Okra' from Harold Courlander: *Terrapin's Pot of Sense*, Holt, Rinehart & Winston 1957. Copyright 1957, 1985 by Harold Courlander. There are many versions of this tale of breaking bad news, including one by Joseph Jacobs in *More English Fairy Tales*, David Nutt 1894.

'Noodle Bug' by Roger McGough from *after the merrymaking*, Jonathan Cape 1971. Reprinted by permission of A D Peters and Co., Ltd.

9

'Jack and the Devil' Black American. Collected by Zora Neale Hurston: *Mules and Men* (J B Lippincott Co. Inc.). Slightly adapted.

'Jim Buckey, Strong Man' Collected by Herbert Halpert: *California Folklore Quarterly* 1945 and reprinted in Tristram P Coffin & Hennig Cohen (eds): *Folklore from the Working Folk of America* Doubleday (Anchor Books) 1974. Adapted.

'The Fast Fencers' from Bill Wannan: *Fair Go, Spinner*, Lansdowne Press. Reprinted by permission of Curtis Brown (Aust.) Pty. Ltd., Sydney.

'Crooked Mick goes for a Job' from Bill Wannan: *Crooked Mick of the Speewah*, Lansdowne Press 1966. Reprinted by permission of Curtis Brown (Aust.) Pty. Ltd., Sydney. Adapted. Crooked Mick — he got his name because one of his legs buckled in the heat when he was out on the Speewah one day — is the Australian legendary hero of the sheep stations, the equivalent of Paul Bunyan among lumberjacks and Pecos Bill of the American West. The Speewah Sheep Station is similarly larger than life. In summer the days are so hot that freezing point is fixed at 99° and the nights are so short that there are only 40 minutes in an hour. It is plagued by huge mosquitoes, giant wombats, flocks of galahs so dense they prevent any rain, should it ever fall, from reaching the ground, hoop snakes, oozlum birds, and so on.

'The Sissy from Anaconda' by Stewart Holbrook. Recorded by B A Botkin, from *American Testament, The Story of a Promised Land* (Grace Books 1956).

10

'The Hickory Toothpick' by Percy MacKaye: *Tall Tales of the Kentucky Mountains*, George H Doran, Co., 1926. I have taken and slightly adapted it from Richard Chase's *American Folk Tales and Songs*, New American Library, 1956 where he notes that the tale is from near Pine Mountain in Eastern Kentucky and that MacKaye 'wrote it up as told by Old Sol Shell'.

'Water in the Gourd' from Eddie Burke & Anne Garside (eds): *Water in the Gourd and Other Jamaican Folk Stories*. © OUP 1975

'The Year of the Big Freeze' from Stephen Dow Beckham: *Tall Tales from Rogue River: the Yarns of Hathaway Jones* (Indiana University Press 1974). Reprinted by permission of the author.
'Hot' from Harold Courlander: *A Treasury of Afro-American Folklore*, Crown Publishers Inc. 1976. Adapted.

11

'Plenty Rations is Comin'' Black American Collected by Zora Neale Hurston: *Mules and Men* (J B Lippincott Co. Ltd.). Slightly adapted. Similar stories of hunting prowess have been popular at least since Raspe's Munchausen tales 200 years ago and are frequently attributed to legendary heroes like Paul Bunyan and Crooked Mick. The following Scottish version, from Alexander Lowson: *Tales, Legends and Traditions of Forfarshire* (Forfar 1891), is included in David Buchan: *Scottish Tradition*, Routledge & Kegan Paul 1984:

> Dan was bragging of some fine sport he had one day shooting gulls in the Brandy Cove. 'Ye ken naething about shootin',' cried the Deacon. 'I min' aince on a time o' firin' at a covey o' partricks, oot gaed my shot, it killed three hunner o' th' brutes, an' my ramrod gaed aff wi' the shot, gaed two mile i' th' cluds, and stringed seven wild geese, a' sailin' in a troop, by th' een, the shot wis sae strang, the gun puttit me, ower I gaed, an' killed a fat hare i' the seat, an' as I wis tryin' tae get up I put my taes i' the yird and I kicked twenty pints o' honey oot o' a foggy bees' byke — that wis a shot tae blaw o'.'

'Crooked Mick the Hunter' from Bill Wannan: *Crooked Mick of the Speewah*, Lansdowne Press 1966. Slightly adapted. Reprinted by permission of Curtis Brown (Aust.) Pty. Ltd. Sydney.
'Cougar Tamer' from *Idaho Lore* reprinted by B A Botkin. See the note on 'A Family Pet'.
'A Snake Yarn' by W T Goodge. A swagman was an Australian ranch worker who travelled from one sheep station to another. Round the equipment (swag) that he carried, he rolled his 'bluey', a grey-blue blanket.

12

'Fearsome Critters' Retold from material in Charles Edward Brown: *Paul Bunyan Natural History* (reprinted in B A Botkin: *A Treasury of American Folklore* Crown Publishers 1944); Bill Wannan: *Crooked Mick of the Speewah* Lansdowne Press 1966; and R M Dorson: *Man and Beast in American Comic Legend*, Indiana University Press 1982
'The Snakebit Hoehandle' is a traditional story from the Southern Appalachian mountains. There are many tall tales of the effects of snake bites, especially the bite of the deadly hoop snake. Sometimes they were reported as straightforward fact. John Lawson, in his *History of North Carolina* (1714), writes:

> Of the horn snakes, I never saw but two that I remember. They are like the rattlesnake in colour, but rather lighter. They hiss exactly like a goose when anything approaches them. They strike at their enemy

with their tail (and kill whatsoever they wound with it),
which is armed at the end with a horny substance, like
a cock's spur. This is their weapon. I have heard it
credibly reported, by those who said they were eye-
witnesses, that a small locust tree, about the thickness
of a man's arm, being struck by one of these snakes at
ten o'clock in the morning, then verdant and
flourishing, at four in the afternoon was dead, and the
leaves red and withered.

'Cockatoos on the Speewah' by Alan Marshall in *Australasian Post* 21st June 1951. Reprinted from Bill Wannan (ed): *The Australian*, Rigby Ltd 1954. Reprinted by permission of Curtis Brown (Aust.) Pty. Ltd., Sydney. See the note on 'Crooked Mick goes for a Job'.

'Fur Trout' by Robert Scott © 1987

'The Big Wolf' from *Idaho Lore* reprinted by B A Botkin, where it is called 'Big as an Idaho Potato'. See the note on 'A Family Pet'.

'Mosquitoes in Australia' from Fred J Mills: *Square Dinkum*, reprinted in *The Australian*, Bill Wannan (1954, 1963). Adapted.

'. . . And America' a traditional tale from Tennessee. Tall stories about mosquitoes are many and widespread. One tells how Paul Bunyan brought some very nasty bees to his logging camp in an effort to keep down the mosquitoes but they interbred so he only succeeded in creating an even more vicious insect, one with a sting at *both* ends.

'The Wonderful Ointment' from Will H Robinson: *Yarns of the Desert* Copyright 1921 William Henry Robinson Phoenix, Arizona: The Berryhill Company. I have taken it from B A Botkin: *A Treasury of American Anecdotes* (Random House, 1957), where it is called 'The Growing Salve'. Slightly adapted. Reprinted by permission of Curtis Brown Ltd.

13

'Skunk Oil's Punkin' Collected by Roger L Welsch and printed in his *Treasury of Nebraska Pioneer Folklore*. Copyright 1966 by the University of Nebraska Press and reprinted with their permission. Slightly adapted.

'Paul Bunyan's Cornstalk' by Alastair Graham, based on a tale collected by Harold Courlander.

'The Crookest Raffle Ever Run in Australia' by Frank Hardy from *The Yarns of Billy Borker*. Reprinted by permission of Reed Methuen Publishers Ltd. Slightly adapted.

'Uncle Jasper and the Watermelon Bet' is a traditional Black American story.

'A Narrow Escape' by Henry Lawson. From *Short Stories in Prose and Verse*, Sydney 1894. Slightly adapted.

Every effort has been made to trace and contact copyright holders but this has not always been possible. We apologise for any unintentional infringement of copyright and will rectify this in future editions.

A Narrow Escape

A few years ago I was travelling with a prospecting party in some place and one morning I awoke and found my horse gone. Without disturbing my companions I took a bridle and started to follow up the horse's tracks across the sand.

The horse must have broken loose some time in the night, for I followed his tracks a good distance until they disappeared in a grass patch. I wandered about for some time in a vain endeavour to pick up the trail, and ended by getting lost myself.

The morning passed away, and I was still wandering hopefully, when about noon, I descried three dark figures on the horizon of the plain. I soon saw that they were blacks, and that they were coming in my direction. As they advanced nearer I saw that one was armed with a nulla nulla or club, whilst the other two carried spears which they brandished in an unpleasant manner. I knew there was not a moment to lose if I wished to save my life — which I did — so I started to run. It was an awful race. I felt my underclothing sticking to my body with the perspiration, and my braces and bootlaces gently giving out.

I kept on under the broiling heat, with the blacks steadily gaining in the rear, until at last I felt that I could run no longer. My time was come. I fell on the glistening sand and prayed for a sudden and comparatively painless death.

They came up and surrounded me, and I saw in their looks that I could not expect mercy at their hands. The memories of my life went through my brain like a flash of lightning, or rather like flashes of lightning. The two who were armed with spears raised their weapons to a horizontal position and aimed the points at my heart.

They swayed the spears backward and forward several times to gain momentum. The suspense was very trying indeed. I drew a long breath and attempted to close my eyes; but just as they swung their spears back for a final and fatal thrust the one who carried the club, and who up to this moment stood perfectly still and silent, suddenly raised his weapon and brought it down on my head with a sickening crash, and I fell at his feet a ghastly corpse.